THE CASE OF THE GONE GOOSE

THE CASE
OF THE
GONE GOOSE

by SCOTT CORBETT

Illustrated by Paul Frame

An Atlantic Monthly Press Book
LITTLE, BROWN AND COMPANY
BOSTON   TORONTO

SECOND PRINTING

ATLANTIC–LITTLE, BROWN BOOKS
ARE PUBLISHED BY
LITTLE, BROWN AND COMPANY
IN ASSOCIATION WITH
THE ATLANTIC MONTHLY PRESS

Published simultaneously in Canada
by Little, Brown & Company (Canada) Limited

PRINTED IN THE UNITED STATES OF AMERICA

By Scott Corbett

Susie Sneakers
Midshipman Cruise
Tree House Island
Dead Man's Light
Danger Point
  The Wreck of the Birkenhead
Cutlass Island
One by Sea
What Makes a Car Go?
What Makes TV Work?
What Makes a Light Go On?
The Lemonade Trick
The Mailbox Trick
The Disappearing Dog Trick
The Limerick Trick
The Baseball Trick
The Case of the Gone Goose

THE CASE OF THE GONE GOOSE

1

Inspector Tearle wanted to pace the floor of his summer office, but he couldn't. He would have fallen out of the tree.

Roger Tearle's room, second floor rear in the family home, was his winter office. His summer office, twenty feet from his window and on approximately the same level, was situated in a tree house.

He and his sister Shirley and Thumbs Thorndyke had built it in the big oak tree in the back yard. It was probably the only tree house in the country with a two-drawer steel filing cabinet in one corner.

On the files stood a telephone whose black wire ran over to the house and down to a kitchen window. The phone squawked. He picked up the receiver. He had been expecting this call.

"Inspector Tearle speaking."

"You didn't finish your milk, Inspector."

He sighed.

"Okay, Mom, I will before we leave."

He knew she would call, and he was not in the mood for milk. He was too preoccupied with the Case of the Missing Watch. In fact, it was the Chilton Watch Case that made him want to pace the floor.

Roger Tearle had been given the nickname of "Inspector" by residents of his sometimes grateful village of East Widmarsh. He was also referred to as Roger Tearle the boy bloodhound, Roger Tearle everybody's detective force, and Roger Tearle the nosiest kid in town. In a more general sense he was sometimes called Roger Tearle the human dynamo, the Boy with a Thousand Interests.

As Mr. Chadburn put it one morning down at the post office, while waiting with various village loafers for the mail truck to arrive, "You've got to give that lad credit, he hasn't wasted any of his twelve years. He's lived them to the hilt, every minute of them." And as usual when Mr. Chadburn spoke, there was general agreement, because Mr. Chadburn was a millionaire financier and chicken-fancier who owned Hessian Run Farm and went into the city two or three times a week to make another million dollars.

Only Mervin Stubbert had given the statement a sour reception. Mervin was the village constable, and like many unimaginative professional police officers he resented the efforts of brilliant amateurs. It was he who had labeled Roger the nosiest kid in town. It annoyed Constable Stubbert that it was usually Roger rather than himself who found anything that was missing in East Widmarsh, from a campstool [1] to a small child.[2]

It was scarcely seven o'clock as Inspector Tearle stood in the middle of his summer office with his hands behind his back, staring abstractedly at the filing cabinet. He was an early riser, especially when he was working on a case.

Presently he transferred his stare to his electric wristwatch, which he had won in a magazine subscription contest. He took it off his wrist. He strapped it on again.

[1] The Grimshaw Campstool Case. Inspector Tearle found Miss Grimshaw's missing campstool under a tree in Mr. Chadburn's north meadow. From certain bright-colored splashes on low-hanging leaves and on the ground, he concluded that someone painting with watercolors had borrowed the campstool from the back porch of old Miss Grimshaw's cottage to sit on while doing a landscape of the Widmarsh hills. This was later proved true when it was learned that an arty girl had spent the weekend at Sarah Gourley's guest house on Catawpa Street and had been seen coming back Saturday afternoon with a watercolor of the Widmarsh hills which Sarah said was pretty poor if you asked her.

[2] The McDermott Small Child Case. In this instance, chubby little Ickie McDermott, age three, had apparently wandered away from the back yard of the McDermott residence on Gibbet Lane. While the townspeople, led by Constable Stubbert, were scratching themselves up searching the dense woods across from the McDermott residence, Inspector Tearle had noticed some small sticky footprints in the side yard. The trail led to a utility shed Mrs. McDermott used as a laundry room. There he found evidence that enabled him to quickly close the case. Having somehow got hold of a large jar of honey, Ickie had carried it out to the side yard, eaten a good portion of it, covered himself with it from head to foot, and then managed to let himself into the laundry room, which nobody would have thought he could do. Inspector Tearle found him there, sound asleep in a basket of clean laundry.

He took it off. Put it on again. All the time studying his own movements.

A screech from the street below shattered his train of thought and reminded him he must grease Thumbs Thorndyke's bike brakes. Thumbs never got around to that sort of task himself, and a good thing it was, too. If he had, he would have gotten lots of grease on the wrong places and very little on the right places. Thumbs's nickname was short for "All Thumbs," and he was just that. He was as awkward about doing things as Roger was competent. But he was a stout fellow, meant well, and took orders cheerfully because of his unbounded admiration for Roger's awesome abilities and formidable mental powers.

"Hi, Thumbs."

"Hi, Roger. Time we were getting out to Chadburn's."

Roger glanced at his electric wristwatch again.

"So it is. I'll be right down."

Opening the file, he took out the worksheet for that day's egg route, put it in his pocket, and dropped like a spider monkey down the ladder to join his friend.

He had just wheeled his bicycle out of the shed, holding a one-finger gob of grease clear of the handlebars as he did so, when a tall Amazon of a girl burst out of the back door.

"Wait for me! And Mom says she doesn't want to tell you again to finish your milk!"

6

Purely out of habit, Roger and Thumbs exchanged a disgusted glance. They had long since given up any hope of shaking off Shirley. They had to let her come along.

For one thing, she was Roger's twin sister, even though they did not look much alike. For another, she was an awful tomboy who didn't like to play with girls and never took the suggestion that she go do so. For a third thing, she was so big and strong she could have beaten them both up if they refused to let her come.

At her age, many girls are taller and bigger than the boys in their class. They shoot up like dinosaurs, and for a year or so they tower over all the boys, until suddenly the boys start to grow big and tall and shoot past *them.* But for the present, Shirley was the tallest of the three by half a head, and they had to make the best of it. Shirley was simply one of those things you got used to, like a wart on your nose.

"Hi, Shirl," said Thumbs in a groaning tone of voice.

"Hm, Thmmms," replied Shirley, having just stuffed half of her last piece of breakfast toast into her mouth. While Roger greased Thumbs's brakes and then cleaned his finger on the grass, she fetched her bike from the shed. What a fuss she had made when her parents insisted she have a girl's bike! "Who ever wears a skirt?" she protested.

"Go drink your milk . . . I don't see why he makes such a fuss about finishing one little old glass of milk, anyway," observed Shirley, who had just finished four of them. Roger dashed inside, drank the stuff too fast to suit his mother, and dashed back again.

Together they pedaled off through the fresh morning air down the sun-dappled, tree-lined street. The slanting rays gave them long skinny shadows to race down the street beside them, and the skinniest of the shadows was Roger's. Lean as a greyhound, knobby as a grasshopper, energetic as an ant, he leaned forward like a racer on his bike, desperately eager as always to get to the next place he was going.

He had an often woebegone face that was at odds with his generally cheerful disposition. This was because his eyebrows and eyes both slanted down at the outside cor-

ners (the very opposite, for example, of those of Kiddo Nockamura, the Chadburns' Japanese cook). It was his sad eyes and his wide mouth that also drooped at the corners, combined with his amazing ability to search out things, that had caused Old Sarge to give him the "boy bloodhound" nickname. Old Sarge was the Chadburns' gardener and handyman, and owed his own nickname to his participation in World War I.

By the time they reached Mr. Chadburn's private back road across the north meadow of Hessian Run Farm, Roger began to slow down. He was thinking. The Chilton Watch Case was still on his mind.

"Soon as we finish delivering eggs, I want to go by and see Amos Chilton again," he said. "I'm beginning to get a theory about his watch."

"What kind of theory?"

"I'm not satisfied with his story about not putting his watch on any more after he came in from his bird-walk along the canal towpath. I want to go over that part again."

"But he's sure he never put it on, and he has his sunburn to prove it," Shirley pointed out.

"Even so," murmured Inspector Tearle, "even so . . ."

"I'll bet old Roger will find that watch yet," said Thumbs loyally.

"I hope so. But I'm tired of just finding things. I'm tired of campstools and watches," revealed Roger, and added a wistful wish. "I wish a *real* case would turn up, like the ones the big detectives get."

Among the stacks of books he managed to devour, despite his countless other activities, were all the major works of detective fiction. The methods of Maigret, Poiret, Lord Peter Wimsey, Sherlock Holmes, and even 007 were familiar matters to him and had often helped him in his own investigations. Knowing this, Thumbs and Shirley both looked at him with a high degree of horrified excitement.

"You mean, you wish someone in East Widmarsh would get *murdered?*" Shirley asked in a hushed voice. Hushed for her, at any rate, though for anybody else it would have been a pretty loud voice.

With some reluctance, Roger shook his head.

"No, not really. I mean, I can't think of anybody in East Widmarsh I'd really like to see murdered," he admitted, "not even You Know Who."

"Nor even You Know Who Else," added Shirley, mentioning another villager besides You Know Who that they all had reason to dislike.

"No, I wouldn't want a murder," said Roger, "but . . . Oh, well, I guess I'll have to be satisfied with campstools and wristwatches until I'm older. Only, by then, I'll probably get into science or something and never have time to be a detective!"

He shook his head sorrowfully at the impossibility of doing everything in one lifetime, even though he came closer to making the grade than anybody else in town, if not in the whole county.

One thing Thumbs had was keen ears. Big ones. Sort of like radar dishes, they were. As the threesome rode across the lush green meadow where dew still sparkled on the grass, he noticed something.

"Hey, it's funny, I can't hear any cackling. Wind must be wrong."

Usually, as they approached the beautifully kept showplace of a farm (it was Mr. Chadburn's pride and plaything), they could hear the prize roosters crowing and the exotic hens cackling and the pedigreed geese honking in a regular barnyard symphony. When the wind was right, the three big geese, Tom, Dick, and Harry, could be heard clear in the village, especially by crabby old Uncle Willie Jones, who objected. For that matter, nobody liked those geese much, not even the boys and Shirley. They were noisy and ill-tempered, and inclined to attack anyone who came near. But especially were they noisy. It did indeed seem as if the wind must be wrong that morning. But Roger quickly disposed of such a notion.

"No, the wind is straight out of the southwest at six miles an hour." He always checked his homemade weather station (inside and outside thermometers, barometer, relative humidity indicator and wind velocity gauge) the minute he got out of bed. He had to, in order to enter his findings in the log he kept as a volunteer weather-watcher assisting the U.S. Weather Bureau station at a nearby airport. He stood very high with Mr. Churp, the head meteorologist there.

"Six miles isn't much wind, but still we ought to hear them," Roger added.

"Something's wrong. I feel it in my bones," said Shirley. Her specialty was feminine intuition. It was one of the few ways in which she admitted to being a female. She always insisted she could "feel" things.

Two big barns blocked their vision, as far as getting any glimpse of the poultry yard from the back road was concerned. As they came nearer, they began to hear the cackle chorus, but in a muffled way, as if from inside the henhouse.

The road curved between the barns, and then the important features of the place came into view. The big poultry yard and the long, low henhouse, so fancy it looked like a high-class motel. The tenant farmer's house. The paddock. The vegetable garden. The cut flower garden. The tennis court. The swimming pool. The big, rambling Colonial farmhouse, carefully and lavishly restored. Through the trees, a tip of the roof of Old Sarge's prefabricated cottage. But none of the three cyclists had eyes for any of these details that morning, because something was definitely wrong at Hessian Run Farm.

The poultry yard *was* empty of chickens, ducks, and geese, with one sinister exception.

Standing in a circle inside the large, well-fenced en-

closure where the prize fowls usually scratched and strutted were four men. They were Mr. Chadburn, Kiddo Nockamura, Old Sarge, and Zoltan Dubrovnic, the Hungarian tenant farmer.

"What are they looking at?" wondered Thumbs. But his wonderment was nothing as compared to the burning curiosity that immediately flamed through Inspector Tearle. Skidding his bike to a stop, Roger raced to the fence.

"What's up, Mr. Chadburn?"

The millionaire financier and chicken-fancier was a short, stout, red-faced little rooster of a man, with a rooster's temper. When he was home, he usually wore faded farm clothes, but this morning he was wearing his city clothes. At the sound of Roger's shrill, excited voice, both he and Kiddo turned, breaking the circle enough to give Roger an unobstructed view of what lay inside it.

He took one look, and turned pale. Despite the condition of the goose, Roger knew which one it was. He swallowed hard, then shook off his momentary giddiness enough to spin around and give Thumbs and Shirley his opinion.

"It's Tom," he declared, "and he's been *murdered!*"

2

"*Murdered?*" cried Shirley.

"*Murdered?*" cried Thumbs.

"Yes, murdered," said Roger. "His . . ." He gulped before he could continue. "His head's been chopped off!"

Shirley gasped.

"I can't even see the head," Roger went on, "but I can tell it's Tom."

"That funny-colored left foot?"

"Yes."

"But who would do a thing like that?"

A strange, eager light began to glow in Inspector Tearle's sadly slanted blue eyes.

"I don't know, but I can think of a list of suspects as long as your arm."

"But why Tom? If you ask me, Dick is the nastiest one."

"That's your opinion, Shirley. Maybe someone else felt different."

"I always thought Harry was the worst," said Thumbs.

"See?" said Roger. "Come on, let's go inside."

They raced along the fence to a gate, let themselves in, and joined the group around the body. On the way they saw the head, lying some distance away.

"That's Tom, all right," said Shirley.

"Sure it is."

The men were talking angrily.

"It's vandalism, that's what it is, plain vandalism," Old Sarge was saying. "I'm blamed if I can see why anyone would take the trouble to come out here and chop off a goose's head, less'n he was sick in his own head."

"Lots of people around these parts aren't fond of our geese," snapped Mr. Chadburn. "Always complaining about the noise. Your fine friend Uncle Willie has threatened to shoot them more than once. Sometimes I'm tempted to stop selling that old coot any eggs, I get so tired of his crabbing."

Old Sarge looked outraged. His straggly gray mustache did its best to bristle at this insult to his cribbage crony.

"Now, Junior, you know Willie was just talking," he protested. He spoke very freely to Mr. Chadburn, because he had been his father's sergeant in World War I and had been like part of the family ever since. "Besides, Willie wouldn't come traipsing out before dawn in the cold night air, not with his rheumatism, and that's when this job must have been done, right at dawn, when the door went up and Tom could get out. Anyways, Willie said shoot, not chop."

Mr. Chadburn shook his head.

"I'm not saying he did it, I'm just saying he's an example, the first one that comes to mind, of the many people around here that don't like our geese."

With his ears tuned to the conversation, Inspector Tearle prowled around the edge of the circle, examining the ground. Then he stopped to ask a question.

"Mr. Chadburn, are you going to call in Constable Stubbert?"

The millionaire chicken-fancier snorted.

"I should say not. I don't want him messing around here, trampling down the flowers."

Roger beamed his approval of this decision.

"Then can I investigate?"

"Sure, sure, but what I specially want you kids to do is to take this bird and get rid of it for me. I want it off the place before Mrs. Chadburn comes out, because she can't stand the sight of blood. Zoltan, put it in a sack for them. Take it to the Plummingtons, or have your mother cook it herself if she wants to. Make a darn fine meal for somebody, but nobody here on the place is willing to eat it."

"Goose don't agree with me," muttered Zoltan, who always looked as if very little of anything agreed with him. Many Hungarians are said to be gloomy-looking, especially when playing their native instruments, but Zoltan overdid it without even playing anything.

"What about our eggs?" asked Roger.

"Not ready yet. This business threw everything off schedule around here, when Zoltan came running with the news. Take care of Tom, and come back for the eggs later."

"Wait!" cried Roger, as Zoltan bent to pick up the goose. "Let me mark the position the body was found in."

Grabbing a stick, he quickly drew a line around the body, while Mr. Chadburn shook his head with a half-exasperated, half-amused grin, and Kiddo watched po-

litely, and Old Sarge guffawed, and Zoltan muttered. Then Zoltan took Tom away, and brought him back neatly wrapped and stuffed into a big shopping bag. Just in time, too, because as Roger put the package in his wire basket and they pedaled off, Mrs. Chadburn could be seen a hundred yards away, coming out of the house.

As they wheeled across the north meadow again, Inspector Tearle was trembling with a fierce kind of joy.

"How do you like that?" he exulted. "I've got a murder case!"

"A goose!" scoffed Shirley.

"What difference does that make?" snapped Roger. "Murder is murder. First thing we've got to do, soon as we get a chance, is draw up a list of suspects."

"It'll be a regular telephone book," said Thumbs.

"I know. The second thing we'll have to do is start trying to eliminate some."

Moments later they were home again.

"Mom! Can you come out a minute?"

Neat in a crisp lemon-yellow apron, Mrs. Tearle appeared on the back steps.

"What is it?"

They took turns interrupting each other to bark out the news. She looked properly astonished.

"And, Mom, I'm in charge of the investigation! He's not going to call in Constable Stubbert to trample down their flowers," Roger reported triumphantly. "Mr. Chadburn said we're to give Tom to the Plummingtons . . .

or he said you could cook him yourself, if you wanted to."

The Plummingtons were a large family whose father was nice and amiable, but not fond of working. The whole village was used to helping them out. Mrs. Tearle cocked a twinkling eye at the large package in Roger's basket.

"My! Imagine having a celebrity for supper! I don't see why we shouldn't enjoy him ourselves!"

Brother and sister exchanged a startled glance.

"Gee, I wouldn't want to eat a goose I knew personally," declared Shirley. Her mother was impressed. The fact that there was anything that Shirley didn't want to eat was news indeed. But she continued to have her fun.

"Oh, nonsense, Shirley! Why, roast goose is delicious!"

Roger squirmed on his bike seat.

"Aw, come on, Mom!"

"Well, what's wrong? You could be the first detective who ever sat down and ate the victim!"

Roger looked at her and began sheepishly to grin. He should have known she was teasing, but sometimes when he was intent on a case his sense of humor got lost for a minute. Mrs. Tearle laughed.

"Well, all right, if you want to pass up a chance like that, go ahead and take him over to the Plummingtons."

The Plummingtons lived alongside the canal on the other side of town in an ancient, rugged stone building that had once been a mill. Flour had been ground there

clear back in Colonial times. The town fathers had their eyes on the mill for a historical landmark, if they could ever get the Plummingtons out of it.

On a jerry-built front porch, in a rickety wicker arm-chair, sat Mr. Plummington. Out in the bare front yard seven or eight of his younger children were happily at play. He almost got up when Roger handed him Tom, he was so surprised, especially when they told him what had happened. He thanked them kindly, and turned the goose over to his wife with instructions to take it out in back and pluck it.

This errand accomplished, Roger remembered his intention to stop by Amos Chilton's printing shop. They returned at top speed to the village square, threading their way expertly through its slight traffic.

"We can't let the Watch Case go just because we're working on something bigger now," Roger pointed out as they swerved into the parking lot behind the shop and stacked their bikes against a wall. "From now on we'll have to juggle things."

Amos Chilton was busy at one of the Miehle presses, turning out a Chamber of Commerce circular. Roger greedily sniffed the printer's-ink aroma of the shop. Mr. Chilton, a tall, round-shouldered man, had been promising to teach him how to set type sometime but was always too busy to get around to it. His head bobbed in one of his quick nods as they came in.

"Hi, kids."

"Morning, Mr. Chilton. Found your watch yet?"

He shook his head almost as sharply as he had nodded it.

"Nope. I'd be afraid it's gone for good if it weren't that it *has* to be around the house somewhere. There's no way it could have got out. I've been through all the trash, and everything."

"Hmm. Well, I just wanted to ask you a few questions again."

"Fire away."

Roger whipped out a pocket notebook and opened it to his notes on the Watch Case.

"You had your watch when you went for that bird-walk along the canal on Saturday. We know that because you got sunburned, and the watch left a band of white skin on your wrist."

"That's right. My sunburn's beginning to itch, too," said Mr. Chilton irritably, stopping to scratch. "I think it's going to peel on me."

"You came home from your walk," Inspector Tearle continued patiently, "and you know you took it off then, because you had to shave to go to the Bilsop wedding, and you always take it off when you shave."

"That's right. And that means it's got to be some-where around the house, because I never put it on again. If I'd put it on again, I'd have lined it up with the white mark on my wrist — anybody would naturally do that — and if I'd done that I'd remember doing it."

"You were hurrying to get ready for the wedding."

"Yes, I was a little late, and Mrs. Chilton was jawing at me."

"You're sure that in the rush you didn't grab your watch and put it on again?"

"Sure I'm sure! Like I just told you —"

"Yes, sir. I just wanted to make sure."

Mr. Chilton looked down at him belligerently.

"But you still don't believe it," he charged.

Inspector Tearle shrugged.

"Well, you've looked in every possible place you can think of. So when you look in all the possible places and something's not there, then you have to start looking in the impossible ones."

"Hmp! Well, I wish you luck, Inspector, but I think you're barking up the wrong tree. Makes me mad, though. It was a fine watch. And I'd just bought a new band for it, too!"

"Well, don't give up yet, Mr. Chilton. See you later."

Pausing only for one last whiff of printer's ink, Roger hurried his associates outside to their bikes.

"We'll pick up the mail and drop it by the house, and then we've got to get back out to the farm," he declared. "Zoltan ought to have the eggs ready by now, and everybody will be wondering why we're late. Besides, I want to go over the scene of the crime before every clue has been destroyed!"

3

THE MORNING mailbag for the Tearle household was on the light side. For Roger there were a circular from a firm that made telescopes, a letter containing a set of Tanzanian commemoratives sent on approval by a stamp company, a weekly bulletin of nationwide contests, a letter from the Chief of Detectives in New York City in answer to a query concerning how his department handled certain routine investigations, a note from their Congressman saying how nice it was to hear from him again and enclosing a copy of a report he had asked for, a couple of advertising leaflets from a magicians' equipment firm and an outfit called Junior Electronics, and a postal chess card from two nuclear physics professors at the University of California at Berkeley, with whom he had been playing chess by mail for over a year now. They played him as a team, and it was generally all he could do to beat them two games out of three.

There was also a letter for his father (a bill), and a postcard for his mother.

Roger clipped the mail into his basket with the postal chess card on top, and glanced down at it as they rode on toward home.

"Hmm. I thought they might fall into that trap in Game Two," he murmured. "Now I can force mate in six . . ."

Shirley ran in with the mail — she wanted to get a few cookies anyway — and then they pedaled off again toward the farm.

On the far side of the north meadow, behind the big cattle barn, was a tree-shaded hollow thick with underbrush. Roger eyed it thoughtfully as they passed.

"Anybody could camouflage a pup tent down in that hollow so that nobody would ever notice it," he remarked, thinking aloud.

"Huh? What are you talking about, Roger?"

"Just an idea, if we need it. I'll tell you later."

Even Shirley had learned not to keep after him when he was thinking something out. They let him alone.

"Dmm fmmgmt," was all she said, which would probably have come out "Don't forget" if she had not had her mouth full of cookies.

There was no lack of cackle now in the poultry yard. All the prize fowls were scratching and clucking, crowing and strutting about, for all the world as though one of their number had not been vilely done away with in that very place a few hours earlier. It was the way of the world. Life goes on. Hissing and honking belligerently, Dick and Harry waddled toward the fence as they approached.

"Oh, quiet!" said Thumbs. "They haven't learned a thing."

The careless footsteps of man and bird had all but obliterated the outline Roger had drawn around the body, but a few traces of the line were still visible. Taking out his retractable steel tape measure, Roger fed the end of it through the fence and along the ground toward the marks. Dick and Harry came over to peck at it viciously.

"Press the release, so it'll wind up fast and give 'em a scare," suggested Thumbs.

"Wait till I get my measurement . . . Thirty-four inches. Now!"

The tape measure suddenly raced backward from under the geese's bills. But instead of being startled, they darted after it, trying for one last peck.

"Those crazy birds," snorted Thumbs. "They're not afraid of anything."

"Maybe that's their fatal misfortune," suggested Roger. He peered in at the ground around the marks. "Darn it, there's one thing I hoped to find, but I didn't see it when we were in there and I don't see it now."

"What's that?"

"The chop mark. There's no chopping block in there, just the ground, so there ought to be a cut in the dirt somewhere. If we could find it and measure it, we could maybe get some idea of the size of the axe or hatchet that was used."

"The murder weapon," said Thumbs, shivering with pleasure.

"Right," said Roger approvingly. "That's the spirit."

"Still only a goose," sniffed Shirley, not yet ready to give up her wet-blanket tendencies, but not managing quite so obnoxious a tone this time. Roger ignored her grandly. He rose from where he had been kneeling, and as he did so noticed something else.

"Look here. Can you see it?" he asked, cocking his

head this way and that as he stared down at the grass in front of the fence.

"See what?"

"This." He traced a rectangle in the air just above the grass. It was slightly crushed down in an area which, when he measured it, proved to be eighteen inches long and twelve inches wide.

"The murderer could have stood right here," said Roger, "and he could have been standing on something."

They looked around everywhere for a box or a platform of some sort, but without results. While they were looking, Old Sarge rambled over.

"What you looking for, Inspector?"

"Anything, Sarge. Everything," said Roger. "When you're looking for clues it's important not to decide what you're looking for ahead of time, but to see what's there."

"You fixin' to find out who killed Tom?"

"I'm hoping to."

"Not much to go on."

"That's right."

Old Sarge, who chewed tobacco, collected a mouthful of liquid ammunition and discharged it over the fence at Dick's bill, missing by very little. Dick pulled his head back and withdrew, hissing indignantly. Old Sarge laughed, and then shook his head.

"Young Chadburn," he said — the old man called the boss that, even though Mr. Chadburn was fifty if he was a day — "Young Chadburn is mighty upset about this. Now he's only got two of them durn geese to show against Gilhuly's at the poultry show next week, and you know they've got that bet on. You wouldn't believe how much money Junior bet him that his geese would take the prize over Gilhuly's. Wouldn't believe it iff'n I told you."

"Five hundred dollars," said Roger.

Old Sarge stopped chewing in mid-chaw.

"How did you know that?"

"I just know," said Roger, who had a detective's normal dislike of revealing the sources of his information. Old Sarge chuckled.

"Not much you *don't* know about what goes on in these parts," he declared admiringly. "Well, you're right, five hundred smackers, and that's not chicken feed. Old Gilhuly has never beaten him yet in any category, and Junior says he won't this time, neither. The Gaines County Poultry Show — by gum, it means a lot to both them fellers."

"I know," said Roger, looking thoughtfully at the two remaining geese.

From the paddock nearby, Thunderbolt whinnied good morning to them. Thunderbolt was Mr. Chadburn's fine saddle horse that he was always too busy to ride but always meant to, because he was getting a bit beefy around the middle and needed the exercise. Mr. Chadburn, that is. Thunderbolt was in fine shape around the middle.

They all walked over to say good morning to him. Thumbs sighed longingly.

"I sure wish Mr. Chadburn would let us ride him once!"

"Me, too!" and "So do I!" said Shirley and Roger.

"Why, shucks, he can't let a bunch of kids ride around on a fine horse like that," declared Old Sarge. "Man alive, how we could have used a mount like Thunderbolt in the old Cavalry!"

Old Sarge often referred to himself as the last of the old Horse Cavalry. He sighed for the good old days, before junk like tanks took over and ruined warfare. He was proud of his days in the service, and had a fine old U. S. Cavalry saber hanging in the sitting room over in his prefabricated cottage. The ancient warrior patted

Thunderbolt on the nose and gave him a lump of sugar he happened to have with him.

"Well, I can't stand here chinning all day, I'd better get over to that lettuce patch and see if Snappy's waiting." Snappy was his name for the little garter snake he claimed kept him company in the garden every day. He marched off, narrowly missing Dick's bill again on his way past. They all laughed, because they knew why Old Sarge had it in for Dick.

Behind them, Zoltan Dubrovnic came stumping out of the utility barn.

"Eggs not ready yet," he muttered, and paused to cough dolefully. Zoltan supposedly had almost everything wrong with him that anybody could have, and what he didn't have, his wife Zaza did have. It was because of Zoltan's health that Mr. Chadburn had installed the special door in the henhouse — that and the fact that he could never resist a new gadget of any kind. The special door was light-controlled. As soon as the first signs of daylight appeared, the door opened, without Zoltan or Zaza having to get up to open it. And always, butting the other fowls to one side, Tom, Dick, and Harry were the first to come out. Now it would be only Dick and Harry. Tom had made his last, his final exit.

"How soon *will* they be ready, Zoltan?" asked Roger.

"Zaza finish putting in boxes soon," muttered Zoltan, and walked on toward his own neat little bungalow to take his mid-morning cough medicine. Other people took coffee breaks. Zoltan took medicine breaks.

Roger glanced around at his assistants and pulled out his pocket notebook and pencil.

"Okay," he said, "this gives us a chance to sit down and work out our list of suspects!"

4

THEY settled themselves comfortably cross-legged in the grass alongside the paddock fence, where from time to time Thunderbolt appeared to be reading over Roger's shoulder.

"All right, now for our suspects . . ."

"Well, personally, I didn't do it," said Thumbs, "but the way I feel is, if anybody had to be murdered, I'm glad it was one of those geese. What if it had been Rocky, or Big Bertha?" he went on, mentioning their favorite rooster and their favorite hen. "That would really have been terrible."

He was right, of course. The chickens were not only their friends but their business associates, without whom they would have been out of the egg business. The hens produced so many eggs that Mr. Chadburn had to do something with the excess. Roger had come up with a profitable solution for everybody, an egg route through the village. Like most millionaires, Mr. Chadburn was never averse to putting a few more dollars into his pocket. "Better mine than someone else's," as he cheerfully put it.

"Well, one thing we do know is, nobody liked those geese," said Roger. "They didn't even like each other. So let's start right here on the farm. Our first suspect is Mr. Chadburn."

The others stared. Then they hooted.

"Mr. Chadburn? Are you crazy? They're *his* geese, his own prize geese! Why would he want to kill them?"

Roger sighed sadly. And when Roger multiplied his normally sad-looking expression by an actually sad expression, he looked very sad indeed. It was sadness squared, so to speak.

"This is why most people can't be successful detectives," he declared. "They can't get it through their heads that you have to keep an open mind and suspect *everybody*. I know it's hard to think of any motive for Mr. Chadburn, but until we're able to find out where he was at the time of the murder and establish his innocence, he has to stay on the list."

Thumbs and Shirley exchanged a glance and shrugged.

"Well, okay, Roger, if you say so."

"Okay. Next, Mrs. Chadburn."

His assistants rolled back on the grass this time, hooting even louder.

"Mrs. Chadburn! Why, she can't even stand the sight of blood!" cried Thumbs. "Mr. Chadburn said so."

"And I know it's so, and so do you. She's the worst scaredy-cat I've ever seen," said Shirley. "Besides, she's nice and loves all animals, even the ones she's scared of. She wouldn't even let Old Sarge kill Snappy."

"Aw, he wouldn't have killed him, anyway," said Thumbs. "He just talks. Why, he's made a regular pet out of him. He says Snappy even comes out now and hangs around watching him work."

"I don't believe it," said Shirley. "That's just his way of keeping Mrs. Chadburn out of the vegetable garden, so's she won't tell him different ways to do things."

Inspector Tearle had been listening to all these side comments with growing impatience. Now he rapped sharply for order.

"All right, all right, any time you two finish your little chat we'll go on. We're not talking about garter snakes, we're talking about murder suspects. Let's stick to the subject."

"Okay, okay. Who's next?"

Roger cleared his throat and took the plunge.

"Our third suspect, of course, has to be Old Sarge."

This got him a combined glare that made even Roger draw back a bit.

"Now, just a minute, you," said Shirley, looking around for something to hit him with. "Don't you go saying things like that about Old Sarge."

Roger sprang to his feet, not only to glower down at them, but also to get out of range.

"Very well! Are we going to be sentimental, or are we going to be objective and scientific — and coldly analytical about it?" he asked, recalling a phrase from his reading. "I don't like it any better than you do, and I'm sure we can clear Old Sarge in short order, but until we do we've got to put him on the list, because he's here on the farm and he *could* have done it. And don't forget one thing. He had a motive."

Shirley and Thumbs did their best to keep glaring, but the old fire was missing. They could no longer meet Roger's gaze squarely. They knew what he was talking about, and looked as if they wished he hadn't mentioned it.

They were all remembering the time Old Sarge had been standing beside the fence and had turned around to pick up a bandana handkerchief that had fallen out of his hip pocket. In bending over he had carelessly allowed the seat of his pants to press against the wire fence.

Dick did not let the opportunity pass. It was said by those who saw it happen that Old Sarge definitely broke the record for the standing broad jump by men over

seventy. He claimed he still had a scar from Dick's atrocious peck, though of course he could hardly go around proving it.

"Well, I don't care," Thumbs said finally, "Old Sarge didn't do it. Why would he kill Tom, anyway? If he was going to kill a goose, he'd kill Dick, not Tom!"

Skinny legs planted apart, hands in the pockets of his shorts, Inspector Tearle pursed his lips thoughtfully.

"Mistaken identification . . . It was just barely getting light out . . . There's all sorts of possibilities . . ."

Thumbs was glaring again, and Shirley was looking around for a heavy object to throw. Roger changed his tune.

"However, there's plenty of other suspects, so let's continue. Next! Kiddo Nockamura."

His timing was good. He had moved on nimbly to the next suspect before the lynching party could get organized. Their outraged expressions faded into troubled stares. But then Shirley shook her head.

"Aw, Kiddo wouldn't do such a thing. He's crazy, but he's all right. And besides, he's devoted to Mr. and Mrs. Chadburn. I heard her say so one day. 'Kito's just devoted to us, and we are to him. He won't even leave us to go back to Japan,' she said." Kiddo's real first name was Kito, but only Mrs. Chadburn called him that. "So he certainly wouldn't kill Mr. Chadburn's own goose when he's devoted to him."

"He hasn't even got pecked, either," added Thumbs.

Inspector Tearle eyed them relentlessly.

"Still, he was there. He had the chance."

"Oh, all right," Shirley conceded in a grudging tone. "Put him on the list."

"Okay. Next, Zoltan."

This offering got a better reception. While they did not dislike Zoltan, there was nothing much to like about him, either. He never really talked, he just muttered, and most of what he muttered was complaints. Though he did have a lot of things wrong with him, there was also the suspicion that he made the most of his ailments in order to get out of work. He was not very nice to poor Zaza. Furthermore, he looked the part of a villain. He had a swarthy face with a scar on one cheek. His greasy black hair hung down in his eyes, causing him to squint in an evil way. He smoked sickening black cigars.

On the other hand, he was the best poultryman in the county. Why would he kill a goose he had taken so much trouble to raise?

All these things went through each of their minds as they considered Zoltan. It was Thumbs who broke the thoughtful silence.

"He'd be crazy to kill Tom. Besides, he wouldn't get up that early if he could help it."

"On the other hand," said Shirley, "maybe he *is* crazy. Write him down."

Roger wrote.

"Okay. Next, Zaza."

They all had to laugh. Fat, dumpy little Zaza. She too was a complainer. She never smiled. She wasn't any nicer to poor Zoltan than he was to her. And she was used to chopping off chickens' heads, if not geese's . . . Still, the only reason she might do it would be to make Zoltan mad. And with so many other ways to make him mad, why should she bother?

"Put her down. But, gee . . . Zaza!" said Shirley, and

laughed again at the picture of fat Zaza chasing fat Tom around the poultry yard with a hatchet.

"Okay, that takes care of the farm. Next, the suspect who lives nearest to the farm and has the best motive."

"You mean . . . ?"

"Yes."

"Uncle Willie Jones?"

"Yes."

Thumbs rubbed his hands together.

"Well, at least he's a pretty good suspect, rheumatism or no rheumatism. Put him down. Who else?"

"Well, we have to put down Person or Persons Unknown, of course."

"Who's that?"

"That's anybody in the village we haven't thought of. In or *out* of the village, I should say. Also, there's the Unknown Vandal."

Thumbs chortled at a sudden thought.

"How about Plummington?" he quipped.

But Roger surprised him.

"You're right, Thumbs. When you're considering suspects, you always have to stop and ask yourself one question. Who stood to gain by the murder? And Plummington stood to gain."

"Aw, but how could he know he did? How could he be sure he'd get the goose after it was killed?"

"I can't imagine him getting up out of that chair and

coming all the way over here for *anything*, let alone a chance on a goose," said Shirley.

"I can't either, but I'll put him down," said Roger, which made Thumbs feel proud in spite of his own doubts as to the suspect's possible guilt.

"Anybody else, Roger?" he asked, resting on his laurels.

"Well, now we have to go outside the village. And the only one I can think of outside the village is Mr. Gilhuly."

"Mr. Gilhuly?"

"That man Mr. Chadburn has the bet with?"

Roger nodded.

"His arch-rival. He's another one who stands to benefit. He knows Mr. Chadburn's poultry have always beaten his at the poultry show. He's probably afraid his geese won't win, and he'll lose the bet."

"Say, that's an idea!"

"He's almost as rich and important as Mr. Chadburn, though, so he probably wouldn't do the job personally," brooded Inspector Tearle. "He'd probably send a hired killer."

"Put him down!" cried Thumbs enthusiastically. "He's a good one! Now how many have we got?"

Roger tallied them up.

"Actual suspects by name, nine. Mr. and Mrs. Chadburn, Old Sarge, Kiddo, Zoltan, Zaza, Uncle Willie, Plummington, and Mr. Gilhuly or his hired killer."

43

He closed his notebook.

"Now we've got to get busy and start seeing who we can eliminate. And I know a good place to start."

"Where?"

"Second stop on our egg route."

Thumbs and Shirley exchanged an excited glance.

"Uncle Willie Jones!"

5

ZOLTAN DUBROVNIC came out of his bungalow, muttering to himself, and crossed the farmyard to the barn where Zaza was presumably finishing the task of boxing the eggs.

Anybody but he might have noticed that three pairs of eyes were following him with unusual intentness, and that they were doing so in silence. But Zoltan seemed unaware of his new glamour. As for the three watchers, they were no longer seeing him as merely Zoltan the Farmer. Now he was Zoltan the Suspect.

He disappeared into the barn. An exchange of irritable Hungarian ensued, after which he reappeared.

"Eggs ready now."

They trooped inside and carried out the eggs. Using old seatbelts scrounged from Jimson's Garage and adapted to their bike baskets, they strapped in the cartons and made ready to go on their Monday rounds.

Thunderbolt whinnied at them, Big Bertha cackled good-by, and Zoltan muttered.

As they wheeled away between the barns and onto the road across the north meadow, Roger glanced once again at the hollow behind the cattle barn. Shirley was quick to notice.

"Why did you say we could hide pup tents there?"

"Because we may want to. I'm not sure yet."

Their first stop was at Miss Grimshaw's cottage. She had lived next door to Uncle Willie Jones for sixty years, but for nearly forty of those years they had not spoken. There was some talk of there having been a lovers' quarrel, but that seemed unlikely, because Miss Grimshaw and Uncle Willie's wife Mabel always spoke. Not Miss Grimshaw and Uncle Willie, however. They were always feuding, but they did their feuding through Mabel. She had to tell each one what the other one had said, even when the other one could hear what was said quite well. And often as not, Mabel sided with Miss Grimshaw.

Before they had even reached Miss Grimshaw's kitchen door, it opened and she poked her head out. It was a small head, sparsely covered with wisps of gray hair, and featured a nose that Uncle Willie had often referred to as a skin-covered paring knife. It *was* long and sharp, true, but not that bad.

"You're late!"

"Yes, ma'am. There was trouble over at the farm."

"Trouble? What trouble?"

"Somebody killed Tom."

"Tom? One of them geese?"

"Yes, ma'am. Somebody chopped his head off."

"Well! I do declare!" The door opened wider. "Come in a minute. I just made some brownies."

Before he could even accept the invitation, Roger was all but butted inside by his sister. Miss Grimshaw passed the brownies and asked more questions.

"When did it happen?"

"About dawn, they think."

"Do declare! Now, who would do a thing like that?"

Miss Grimshaw peered fiercely out her kitchen window in the direction of the house next door and then turned bright gimlet eyes back Roger's way.

"You're looking into this business, I suppose?"

Trying not to seem too pleased by her flattering assumption, Inspector Tearle cleared his throat modestly.

"Well, yes, ma'am, I —"

"Good. You're a bright youngster, you might figger something out." Ever since the Campstool Case, Miss Grimshaw had held Roger in high regard. She squinted out the window again, maliciously. "Well, that does beat all! You don't suppose . . ."

"What's the matter, Miss Grimshaw?"

"I'll tell you a curious thing," she decided briskly. "Now, this is in confidence, and mind you, I'm not accusing anybody of anything, but still it *is* strange . . . I woke up early this morning and couldn't get back to sleep — I have spells of doing that — so I decided to turn on my bedside light and read awhile."

"When was this?"

"About half past three, I'd say. Not long before daylight. But anyway, before I could even turn on my light I happened to glance out the window, and — Of course, I couldn't see much, what with the street lamp being so far up the lane and the town refusing to give us another light pole at this end where it's needed. They can vote money for everything else — new pool table for those hangers-on down at the fire station, more salary for the town clerk —"

"Yes, but what did you see, Miss Grimshaw?" asked Inspector Tearle, nudging her back onto the track.

"What? Oh. Well. I know it was him, too. I'd never miss that ragbag look of his, bundled up in that old coat . . ."

Again Roger tried to conceal his feelings — this time, his excitement.

"You mean, you saw . . . ?"

Miss Grimshaw nodded. She jerked her head toward the window.

"Jones," she snapped. "Now, I don't say he was going out to Chadburn's, and I can't think of what he *would* be going out there for at that hour, though heaven knows he's out there often enough playing cards with that friend of his, but I do know he went past here *in that direction*."

She and Roger exchanged a long stare.

"Did you see him come back?"

"No. Whenever he did, he must have sneaked back by a roundabout way," said Miss Grimshaw in a baldly insinuating tone of voice. Then she folded her hands primly in her lap. "Now, mind, I don't say this has a thing to do with what went on out there in the barnyard, but I do say it's a mighty curious coincidence. Mighty curious. And as I told you, this is just between you and me. I expect you children to keep a confidence. Remember, I'm a good customer."

"Yes, ma'am. We won't tell a soul. And thanks for telling us about it."

They said good-by and, Shirley in particular, accepted a few more brownies. Then they returned to their bicycles in the yard.

It was easier to walk over into Uncle Willie's back yard through a small grove of trees between the cottages than to ride their bikes out to the street and in again on his rutty driveway. Safer for the eggs, too. Unstrapping another carton, Roger headed for the next cottage. His assistants followed, eager for a look at their prime suspect. As they were passing Uncle Willie's woodshed, well back from the house, Roger glanced around, none too pleased.

"If you're going to tag along, don't look so bug-eyed," he ordered. "Act natural!"

In glancing back at them, his eyes were attracted to the open door of the shed. He stopped in his tracks. Sidling over to the door, he looked in. The others were hard on his heels.

Roger's breath rasped sharply. He pointed to the big bark-stripped section of tree trunk Uncle Willie used as

a chopping block. Despite the gloom inside the shed, they could all see it clearly.

Stuck into the top of the chopping block was a hatchet. Roger slipped inside, pulled it free, and examined it. He touched the side of the blade with one finger. Then he turned to the two heads thrust through the doorway behind him.

"It's been wiped off, but not very well," he declared breathlessly. "There's still some blood on it."

Shirley gasped.

"*Sticky* blood?"

Roger nodded.

"Sticky blood!"

6

In her excitement, Shirley forgot all about her former scoffing.

"We've found the murderer!"

But now she was leaning over backwards. Roger pounced on her statement angrily.

"No, we haven't! Stop jumping to conclusions!"

"But he — You said — How can you stand there with the murder weapon right in your hand and say —"

"I say he *may* be the one, but we're a long way from proving it." Roger was beginning to recover from his first flurry enough to have second thoughts. "And who says this is the murder weapon?"

"You said yourself the blood is still sticky."

"Sure. That's what's wrong with it."

"What do you mean, that's what's *wrong* with it?"

"It's been five or six hours since Tom was killed. Would it still be this sticky if it was his blood?"

Shirley hesitated. "Well . . . maybe."

"Maybe not, too." He frowned at the stain. "Maybe if I looked at it under my microscope I could tell if it's goose blood or not, but . . ."

Thumbs added a maybe of his own.

"Maybe Miss Grimshaw put the hatchet there to frame Uncle Willie!"

Roger gazed at him with surprise and approval.

"You're right. That's another thing we should never overlook — the possibility of a frame-up. It comes up all the time. She knew we'd be coming by. She asked me if I was handling the investigation. She knew we'd walk past this shed . . ."

"If you ask me," said Shirley, "that's crazy. Where would Miss Grimshaw get any blood to put on the hatchet?"

From the annoyed looks this brought her, Shirley knew she had taken the wind out of the boys' sails.

"Next you'll be saying Miss Grimshaw trotted out there and chopped off Tom's head herself!" she added, showing them no mercy.

"It's possible," snapped Roger, but he did momentarily look sheepish. He stuck the hatchet back into the block. "Come on, let's get out of here before Uncle Willie comes and catches us. If he *is* the killer, we certainly don't want to put him on guard."

They walked on toward the house. Shirley sniffed the

air. Her sense of smell, sharpened by her insatiable appetite, brought her a news bulletin.

"They're cooking something."

Hearts were beating hard as Roger knocked at the screen door and called, "Eggs, Mrs. Jones!" in a voice that yodeled with tension. Footsteps minced toward the kitchen.

"Well! That you, Roger?" Mrs. Jones chuckled irritatingly. "Sounds as if somebody's voice is changing, I'd say. Why are you so late today? I want to make a cake, and I need my eggs."

"Things got held up over at the farm, ma'am," said Roger. He sniffed. "Something smells good."

"I've got a chicken stewing."

"Fresh-killed, I'll bet, from Swenson's."

"That's right. None of them battery-fed supermarket fowls for me. You might as well cook the plastic wrap as the chicken, far as flavor goes."

They returned past the shed and through the grove of trees to their bikes.

"You see?" said Roger. "Uncle Willie got a chicken from Swenson's farm this morning and killed it himself. So that blood doesn't prove a thing. But nothing has proved he *didn't* do it, either. The big question is, when he went out this morning, did he have the hatchet with him? One thing we've got to do is check that path he takes across the farm to Old Sarge's cottage, and see if we can find any fresh footprints. Hardly anyone uses that path now but Uncle Willie. Let's get going with these eggs — we've got lots of things to do!"

The rest of their route was covered as quickly as possible, with a minimum of conversation along the way. From his silence between stops, Roger's assistants knew he was working up some ideas. After they had delivered their last carton of eggs, he suggested a conference in the tree house. Thumbs gouged his knee climbing up, and Roger issued him an adhesive bandage from a first-aid kit they kept in the steel file. With Thumbs Thorndyke around, it wasn't safe to go anywhere without a first-aid kit. Roger watched Thumbs stanch the blood and cover the wound.

"You know something, Thumbs? You lose a lot of blood in the course of a year. I'm surprised you're not anemic."

When Thumbs had been repaired, they sat down on the airy platform, and Inspector Tearle opened his mind to them.

"First, let's talk about possible motives," he said. "Let's take three of our suspects, Uncle Willie, Zoltan, and Mr. Gilhuly. What's Uncle Willie's motive?"

Shirley eyed him from under straight bangs and over a huge slice of bread and butter she had managed to get her hands on in a detour to the kitchen.

"Thop eeby," she said. Swallowing like a boa con-

strictor, she cleared a large mouthful out of the way. "That's easy," she repeated. "The geese make too much racket to suit him."

"Right. What about Zoltan, Thumbs?"

"Well, it would have to be the same thing with him. He lives closest of all to the henhouse. Maybe they wake him up in the morning."

Roger nodded. "Now, what about Mr. Gilhuly?"

"He's probably afraid he'll lose his bet if he has to show his geese against Tom, Dick, and Harry. I mean Dick and Harry."

"Okay. So what is the one thing all three suspects have in common?"

Roger paused dramatically and, getting no answer, supplied it himself.

"Killing Tom only solved one-third of their problem!"

It took an instant, but not much longer, for this to sink in.

"Say, that's right! Dick and Harry will still make plenty of noise," said Thumbs.

"And Dick and Harry could still win in the poultry show," said Shirley.

Roger nodded again. "You know what I think? I think whoever killed Tom meant to kill all three, but couldn't. Got scared away, or couldn't reach the others, or something. So you can see what that could mean. Bad things come in threes," Roger suggested darkly.

"Why should any of those suspects be satisfied with getting rid of just *one* of the geese?"

"You mean . . . ?"

"Yes. The killer may strike again!"

Their voices had sunk to a whisper now — even Shirley's, and that is saying something — and they glanced over their shoulders down at the yard as they spoke. Even she was thoroughly caught up by the shadowy menace that was now dominating their thoughts.

"That's why I was thinking about that hollow behind the cattle barn," Roger went on. "It would be easy to hide a pup tent under the trees and bushes there. And that's where you and I have got to be tonight, Thumbs."

"Me too!" said Shirley.

"Don't be silly! You can't be in our pup tent."

"I'll bring my own."

"It's no place for girls. It'll be scary," said Roger, but with only the feeblest kind of hope. It was hard to imagine anything that could scare his sister half as much as it would him and Thumbs. Anything bad enough to scare Shirley even a little, he admitted bitterly to himself, would scare them to death.

"Who's scared?" she said. "I'm coming along."

"Oh, let her come," groaned Thumbs. "Just so she brings her own pup tent and stays out of our way."

They glared at her, and then Inspector Tearle resumed his briefing.

"We'd better go out and set up our tents when everybody's busy eating lunch, so let's have ours early and then go out there."

"Good idea!" said Shirley, brushing breadcrumbs off her lap after carefully eating the larger ones. "I'm hungry! Let's go have lunch!"

"Not now!" snorted Roger. He glanced at his electric wristwatch. "It's only half past ten! There's plenty of time to do some work on the Chilton Watch Case first. I want to go over to Mr. Feeney's and ask him if Mr. Chilton bought his new strap from him."

"Well, of course he did," said Shirley. "Who else around here sells them?"

"What new strap?" asked Thumbs.

"Don't you remember? Mr. Chilton said he'd just bought a new band for his watch."

"Oh, that's right. But what do you expect to find out from Mr. Feeney?"

Roger shrugged.

"Who knows? Nothing, maybe. But you have to check everything." He pulled out a letter he had been glancing through while waiting for Shirley to get her bread and butter. "Here, let me read you what the Chief of Detectives in New York City says," he added, and read them a passage that applied to what he had just told them. "So I'm going over to Mr. Feeney's, and if you want to come along, okay."

Naturally they did.

Old Mr. Feeney was a retired jeweler and watch repair-man who still did business in a small way in one corner of his living room. His right eye seemed to stay wider open than his left eye, from all the years he had spent with a jeweler's magnifying lens screwed into it, and his shoulders were rounded from bending over his work. He was a widower and lived by himself, but he puttered around contentedly all day and never seemed to be lonely.

"What can I do for you youngsters?"

"I'm trying to find Mr. Chilton's wristwatch for him, Mr. Feeney."

"That so? Didn't know he'd lost it. Durn shame, it was a fine watch."

"Yes, sir. Did he buy a new strap for it from you?"

"Why, yes, matter of fact, he did. Just last week, as I recall. Cordovan leather, it was, like these here. I particularly remember, because I had trouble with one of the strap pins."

Roger's ears seemed almost to quiver.

"Trouble?"

"Couldn't get one of 'em to hold at first. Spring wasn't working right. But finally I got it to stay. Why did you want to know about the strap, though?"

"Just checking everything, Mr. Feeney," replied Roger. And then, always one to kill two birds with one stone if he could in the course of his busy rounds, he added, "By the way, could you use any eggs? We deliver daily from Chadburn's farm."

Old Mr. Feeney scratched his cheek.

"Well, now you mention it, I might. I don't use too many eggs, and some of them store eggs have gone bad on me since the weather turned hot . . ."

Before they left, Roger had signed up Mr. Feeney for a dozen every Friday.

"Never hurts to ask," he pointed out as they returned to their bikes.

"Where are we going to get more Friday eggs?" demanded Thumbs. "We're selling all the farm can spare now."

"Don't you worry, we'll get the eggs. You know Mr. Chadburn is always looking for an excuse to keep more chickens. I'm sure we can work it out."

"Zoltan won't like it."

"Zoltan doesn't like *anything*, so what's one more thing?"

It was high noon, and almost everybody in East Widmarsh — they hoped — was having lunch. Carrying sleeping bags in their bike baskets and pup tents wrapped around tent poles balanced crosswise, they had ridden across the north meadow and plunged into the hollow. Now they were concealed in a clear space under the trees, where there was room enough to pitch their tents. When they had finished, the two tents could not be seen from the road. In fact, it would have taken extremely sharp eyes to detect them from any side of the hollow whatsoever.

Back on the road again, Roger surveyed the scene with satisfaction. But Thumbs was feeling pessimistic.

"Maybe the killer won't strike again so soon."

"Maybe not. Nobody would expect him to," said Roger, "which is just the reason why he may. Anyhow, we can't take any chances."

"I just know he'll strike again," said Shirley with deep conviction. "I can feel it in my bones."

For a moment Roger was almost glad she was along.

After riding partway back across the meadow, they parked their bikes and picked up the footpath that curved across the meadow and above the gardens and the poultry yard to Old Sarge's cottage. They walked along beside the path, staying off it, so that Roger could study it for footprints. They were not hard to find, nor hard to identify.

"Here, look! You know how Uncle Willie limps a little, because of his rheumatism. He limps like this," said Roger, and imitated his rickety walk. "He comes down harder on the right foot than the left."

"And these footprints are that way." Thumbs pointed to some examples. "The right ones dig in more than the left ones. They're his, all right."

With more than his usual resemblance to a bloodhound, Roger crouched along the trail. They drew even

with the poultry yard, off at a distance of fifty yards or
so to their left, and passed it, with the footprints still
going, dipping through a small hollow. Then Roger
stopped, because the footprints did. They were blurred
and scuffed, as though Uncle Willie had paused and
turned.

"Look!"

Beside them the bank of the hollow was crumbled, as
though Uncle Willie had scrambled up onto it from the
path. Beyond that point the dry grass was too short and

tough for them to make out for sure which way he had gone, or how far. Had he gone over to the poultry yard? What had he done?

Roger sat down on the slope alongside the footprints and stared at them.

"Well, what do you think, Roger?"

His eyes had become blank. He was seeing Uncle Willie limping along the trail in the gray light of dawn. He was hearing the geese waddle outside and begin to honk. He was hearing Uncle Willie stop and swear under his breath . . .

"At least we know one thing," he murmured. "He didn't come over here with the idea of killing any geese."

"No? Why not?"

"If he'd meant to kill them from the beginning, why would he walk this far past them, and then stop and go back?"

"He had a sudden impulse," suggested Shirley.

"But if he had a sudden impulse, he wouldn't have had his hatchet with him." Roger shook his head. "Of course, he still *could* have done it, but I'm beginning to think he didn't. There's another possibility. Maybe he was really on his way to old Sarge's —"

"At four o'clock in the morning?"

"I know. That part's puzzling. But say he was. He hears some funny noises over at the poultry yard. He stops. He goes over for a look."

Roger's sad eyes gleamed.

65

"Maybe *he's* what scared away the killer! Maybe he even saw something — or somebody! Naturally he wouldn't say anything about it, because he wouldn't want it known he was there."

"He'd be afraid they'd think *he* did it!"

"Right!"

They stared at each other. Instead of a solution, they had turned up one more complication. The more they learned, the more the mystery seemed to grow.

7

Dusk was fuzzing the evening air when Roger and his assistants gathered in the Tearle side yard. Parental permission had been given for them to camp out overnight. A few provisions had been packed by Shirley for a late snack. They were ready to go.

"What if Uncle Willie sees us? We have to go right by his house," she pointed out.

"Let him see us. There's nothing funny about our riding out to the farm in the evening. Remember, he probably doesn't even know we're investigating. Miss Grimshaw knows, but you can bet she hasn't told him. If he's sitting out on his front porch, just wave, same as always, and don't overdo it."

Roger was trying to be very matter-of-fact about the whole affair, but he enjoyed a tingling sense of adventure as they pushed off and pedaled down the street where night shadows were already beginning to gather like conspirators under the trees. From his almanac research he knew it was going to be a moonless night, with enough stratus clouds scudding across the sky so that perhaps not even the stars would be shining. A black and moonless night.

When they went by, Uncle Willie was sitting in the swing on his front porch, as expected. Looking grumpy, with his jaw in one hand, he let go of it long enough to return their waves briefly. Was he sitting there plotting further crimes? Or if he wasn't the guilty party, did he know who was?

Through the deepening dusk they rode across the farm. To the south, where the meadow dropped down toward the little stream that was Hessian Run, pockets of fog shrouded the slope and filled in hollows, leaving the tops of small trees to float eerily above. And ahead of them, disconcertingly, their own hollow was a mysterious blob of white that made their legs prickle as they pedaled toward it.

"Would you look at that?" said Thumbs, his eyes somewhat rounder than usual.

Their leader took a deep breath.

"Nothing but ground fog. It'll probably clear away shortly," he declared, with a confidence he did not feel. "Come on, let's go down to our tents."

"If we can find them," grumbled Shirley.

"Let's wheel our bikes down with us and hide them under a bush."

6 8

Cautiously, single file, they picked their way into the hollow. The fog made white ghosts of every tree trunk, and crouching beasts of every bush. Hastily shoving their bikes under cover, they pawed their way toward the tents, which Thumbs found by stumbling over a tent stake that sent him sprawling into the bushes.

Roger zipped open their tent flap, and he and Thumbs crawled in, leaving Shirley crouched wistfully outside the entrance.

"It's not fair," she complained.

Roger had just been waiting for this. He lit a small candle, dispelling the worst of the gray-white darkness.

"You wanted to come," he retorted brutally. "If you don't want to be alone in your tent, you can go home." Then he made a grudging concession. "Oh, well, stick your head in for a minute, till we get our watches set. But just your head."

When they were getting ready for their outing, Thumbs had said he would bring an alarm clock.

"What for?" Roger had asked.

"To wake us up in the morning, in time for dawn."

Roger had snorted.

"Are you crazy? Why not just hang out a sign to tell the killer we're there? Don't you think he'd hear your silly clock, too?"

"Clear behind the barn?"

"Certainly clear behind the barn! How do we know what direction he'll be coming from? He could be walking past right on the road! We can't use any alarm clock, we'll have to set watches."

"Watches? What good will watches do?"

"I mean the kind you stand! Like sentinels or sentries doing guard duty. We'll take turns standing watch, two hours at a time, to make sure we're ready when dawn comes. The first watch can be from ten to twelve, the second from twelve to two, and the last one from two to four. I'll take the first watch."

"I'll take the second," Thumbs had said.

"I'll take the third," Shirley had said, and Roger said okay. Later, when Thumbs asked him, "Are you really going to let Shirl take the third watch?," Roger smiled craftily.

"Of course not, but why argue with her? When you finish your watch, wake me up instead, and I'll take it."

So it was settled. And now Roger reminded them again of the order of their watches.

"Okay, I'll be ready," said Shirley, and opened her sack of provisions. "I'm going to have a sandwich before I turn in."

"I guess I'll have a cookie."

"Me too."

For a while the only sound was the munching of cookies and the smacking of lips. Then, in the distance a whippoorwill called. A whippoorwill's call can be a very melancholy night-sound, especially when a person is sitting in a small tent in a fog-filled hollow. Next, some rustling sounds began, only much closer. Right outside the tent.

"What's that?" cried Shirley, twisting around and pulling her feet under her. Something scurried away into the brush.

Roger's tongue scurried over dry lips.

"Just some small animal. Remember, they're more scared of us than we are of them."

"Then they're pretty scared," croaked Thumbs.

His joke, though delivered in a feeble voice, made them laugh and relieved the tension.

"The heck with it," said Shirley. "*I'm* not scared. I'm going to get in my tent and go to sleep, so I'll be ready for my watch."

With dogged courage the boys could only admire, and taking along the sack of snacks, of course, she pulled her head out of the tent and sprang next door to her own. The zipper on its entrance rasped up and down again so fast that it was hard to believe she could have made it inside without being cut in two. But when Roger called "Okay?" she answered, "Okay."

He turned to his friend.

"You going to keep me company till it's time to start my watch, Thumbs?"

"Sure, I'm not sleepy yet. Let's talk."

"All right, but keep it down. Somebody might come along the road."

It wasn't likely, but somebody might. For a while

they talked about the day's events. But after a time the conversation flagged, and they found themselves listening for night-sounds.

They heard one. It made their hair stand on end.

"WHO-O-O-O-O!"

It was the first indication that there was an owl in residence in the hollow.

When they had recovered from their first fright and realized what the sound was, Thumbs said, "For Pete's sake! Are we going to have *him* around all night?"

"I hope not! I'll bet that scared Shirl silly!"

It was bad enough to hear a hoot like that when you were two in a tent, let alone all by yourself. A surge of big-brotherly feeling flowed through Roger — a rare luxury, since they were not only the same age, but Shirley had been born first and was actually fifty-six minutes older than he. Putting his head near the nylon screening of the entrance, he called softly.

"Hey, Shirl. You okay?"

No answer. Roger cast a manly glance over his shoulder.

"I'm going over and see if she's all right."

He was not eager to stick his head outside their tent, but it was the sort of thing a leader had to do. In his mind's eye was a figure who appeared to be Captain Roger Tearle leaving the trenches to go over the top in Old Sarge's World War I. He crawled outside and forced himself to cover the three feet to Shirley's tent.

A moment later he was back again.

"How do you like that?" he demanded indignantly. "She's sound asleep!"

Thumbs shared his sense of outrage.

"I hate to say it about your own sister, Roger," he declared, "but where there's no sense there's no feeling."

"I hate to say it myself," replied Roger, "but you're absolutely right."

Thumbs was so indignant that he determined to go to

sleep himself, and after considerable thrashing around, he did so. Roger was left alone.

When Inspector Tearle had spoken so glibly of two-hour watches, he had done so without the slightest concern. After all, two hours was nothing. During the late afternoon, for example, two hours had flown by before he had done more than answer the day's mail and take care of a few other routine matters. For one of his busy nature, hours had wings. He had all but forgotten that time could drag.

But now it did.

At first he fought back strongly, determined to make it pass with its usual brisk dispatch. He went over all the suspects again in his mind, one by one. Then he turned to the Chilton Watch Case and analyzed it in the light of Mr. Feeney's evidence. Next he worked out chess moves in his head. He had put out the candle, but had his flashlight close at hand. Presently he checked the time.

Ten o'clock.

Because he had started early, his real two-hour watch was only just beginning. He groaned.

Back he went to chess moves, and from them to algebra problems, and from them to ways to improve the tree house. Next he thought about each of the persons close by on the farm, and wondered what they were doing at that moment. He thought about Dick and Harry, and tried to get excited about the dark menace he felt was hanging over them. One or both might be spending his last night on earth.

He thought about Big Bertha, and Rocky the Rooster, asleep in their chicken motel. He thought about Thunderbolt, taking his ease in his stall. Again and again he was tempted to check the time, but he forced himself to wait until he was sure at least an hour had passed, so that he would know half the vigil was over and he was coming down the home stretch.

Finally, when he felt absolutely sure, he looked at his wristwatch.

Ten-eighteen.

Only eighteen minutes gone! He was crushed. Sitting up in the dark, with his arms around his knees, he was stunned by such a gross betrayal on the part of Father Time. At this rate, two hours began to loom as an eternity.

Worse yet, he was beginning to feel drowsy. His eyes were growing heavy. Startled as he realized the danger that was threatening him, he shook his head and was wide awake again. But not for long. Again his eyelids grew leaden. This time he made his head all but rattle on his shoulders and began to listen hard for night-sounds. What he needed was a good scare that would leave him popeyed with terror. If only there were still a few bears in East Widmarsh! But he knew very well there had not been any around for two hundred years now. Snakes? No poisonous ones within miles. Only nice little fellows like Snappy who wouldn't harm anything but a fly.

The hollow was disgustingly peaceful. Even the owl failed him. Probably off swooping over the meadow, pouncing on some poor innocent little field mouse that never hurt anybody. Roger tried to get mad at the owl, and feel sorry for the mouse, but that didn't work, either. He knew it was a good thing owls did eat up some of the mice. It was Nature's Way.

In desperation he turned to war again. He reminded himself that one of the worst crimes a soldier could commit was to fall asleep while on sentry duty. He recalled stories he had read about Civil War soldiers being shot for that dreadful dereliction of duty. Didn't a mother write to President Lincoln once when her boy was going to be shot?

Roger imagined himself as a Union sentry. Suddenly the hard hand of his colonel was on his shoulder, shaking him awake. He was vaguely surprised to find that the colonel was Mr. Chadburn.

"Private Tearle, I charge you with falling asleep at your post in time of war! Take him away, Old Sarge, and call the firing squad."

Roger found himself being marched off between grim-faced guards to a bullet-pocked wall, while the firing squad came trooping out and took their places. Colonel Chadburn offered him a final cigarette.

"No, thank you, I don't smoke," said Roger, surprised that the millionaire financier and chicken-fancier would offer a cigarette to a twelve-year-old boy, even in the midst of war. He had certainly never done a thing like that before.

Next Colonel Chadburn offered him a blindfold, but Roger waved it away.

"My crime is so low," he said brokenly, "that I don't deserve the smallest consideration. Tell them to fire!"

The rifles were leveled at him, about fifty of them.

"Ready! . . . Aim! . . . Fire!"

Fifty shots rang out. Or at least something rang out. Something went BR-R-R-RING!

Roger's eyes flew open in gray light.

"Roger!"

"Huh? Wha' was 'at?"

"The alarm clock! I snuck it along anyway, just in case!"

"Gugg . . . Wha' time is it?"

"It's after four o'clock. I guess I didn't have it set quite right, but . . ."

Roger had never felt more mortified in all his life. Thumbs might not be brilliant, but his common sense, his extra insurance move, had saved the day. And meanwhile, he, Inspector Tearle, had disgraced himself.

"Gee," mumbled Roger, red-faced, and still trying to fight his way out of a fog of sleep, "I guess I must have dropped off . . ."

"Ssh! Listen!"

Clucks and cackles revealed that the early risers were already afoot in the poultry yard. Stentorian honks announced that Dick and Harry were tuning up for the day.

"Come on," said Roger, sitting up groggily, "we've got to sneak over there to keep watch, and —"

Just then a horrid, extra-loud honk was heard. A sort of goose-scream. It ended abruptly, in a chopped-off way. It was followed by a clattering sound.

"Something's happened!" cried Thumbs, and grabbed the zipper handle to open the tent-flap.

And being Thumbs, naturally he managed to jam the zipper.

"What's the matter? Here! Let me at it!" cried Roger, when he realized what had happened. A moment's struggle and he had the zipper working again, but precious seconds were lost. They tumbled from the tent and scrambled out of the hollow, making no pretense now of trying to creep up on anyone. It was too late for that.

Yes, indeed, far too late. They saw that as soon as they raced between the barns.

Another corpse lay in the poultry yard. Another headless corpse. And no one was in sight, anywhere.

8

THEY peered in through the fence at the corpse.

"Dick," said Thumbs.

"Dick," agreed Roger.

They knew him because he was larger than Harry. He lay about the same distance from the fence that Tom had been.

Though the burden of shame weighed heavily on Roger, who felt his failure keenly, he forced his mind to concentrate on the new problems that faced him. It was no time to be distracted by vain regrets. In the dim early morning light, he peered at the ground narrowly.

"No chop mark again. I don't see one anywhere."

The chickens had drawn away and were huddled together, and they at least had the decency to look upset. But not Harry. Showing no concern for poor Dick at all, he waddled over toward Roger and Thumbs honking angrily, warning them away.

Roger moved along the fence, examining the turf. He pointed to a mark. With the dew still on the grass, it was easy to see. It was a rectangular mark the same as the one he had seen before. This time, however, the back edge was dug sharply into the grass.

"Someone was standing on a box. It tipped over backwards with him, and he fell off. That's the noise we heard, I'll bet anything."

"You going to wake up Mr. Chadburn and tell him?"

"No. I don't want anybody to know we were here, because we may need our hiding place again."

"You mean . . . ?"

"Yes. There's still Harry! Come on, let's get out of sight."

They ran back to the hollow and returned to the tents. Roger peered into Shirley's.

"Wouldn't you know it? She slept right through everything!"

The boys grinned at each other cruelly.

"Won't she be mad when she knows what she missed?"

Savoring this mean thought, they climbed back into their own tent. They had no more than sat down inside when Roger snapped his fingers excitedly.

"I've got it!"

"Got what?"

"The murders weren't done with a hatchet!"

"Huh?"

"No! How could anybody stand on a box on the other side of the fence and chop off a goose's head with a hatchet? Or even an axe?"

"Say! That's true. But then what *was* it done with?"

"I don't know. A sword, maybe, or . . ."

"A sword?"

They exchanged a horrified glance.

"Or maybe a saber!"

Seeing Thumbs's stricken look, Roger hastened to add some welcome words.

"But the box eliminates Old Sarge as a suspect. He's too tall to need any box to stand on."

Thumbs brightened.

"Yeah! So he didn't do it personally, even if it was his saber. . . . Let's see, what about the others?"

"Well, Mr. and Mrs. Chadburn are both short. So is Kiddo. So are Zoltan and Zaza. So is Uncle Willie. And Mr. Gilhuly's hired killer, if he has one, could be either short or tall. The only one that's eliminated for sure is Old Sarge."

"Well, that's something, anyway. How about Plummington, though?"

"I don't know. Have you ever seen him standing up?"

"No."

"Neither have I. But I suppose if he did stand up he'd be pretty tall, or at least not short. I guess he's out, too."

"I never put much hope in him."

"Neither did I. Well, now let's see . . . If Old Sarge didn't do it, could somebody else have borrowed his saber to kill them with?"

"You mean, like for instance Uncle Willie? Say! Suppose he went on over to Old Sarge's yesterday morning, and . . ."

"That's right." Roger looked annoyed with himself. Was he slipping, or what? Here was another mistake he had made! "I shouldn't have jumped to conclusions when we inspected the path. We should have checked to see if any fresh footprints went on to the cottage. He could have gone on over there, sneaked in and got the sword without even waking up Old Sarge, and come back. That would explain why he climbed the bank from a point that side of the poultry yard."

Roger came to a decision.

"We've got to talk to Old Sarge about this. We've got to tell him right out that Uncle Willie was near the scene of the crime yesterday morning. We'll have to check up on where he was *this* morning, too, of course. We've got to see what Old Sarge will have to say about it. If Uncle Willie did it, Old Sarge will know, and his face will give him away. If Uncle Willie didn't do it, but knows something, we've got to find out what it is."

"Okay. So what do we do now?"

As if in answer, from the village came the mellow sound of the church clock striking four. This meant it was now about four-twenty. It was a dependable old clock, never more than twenty minutes slow. Roger stuck his feet into his sleeping bag and stretched out.

"Set the alarm for seven," he said with Spartan determination. "Till then, we might as well go back to sleep."

Nevertheless, it took him quite a while before he could drop off again. Long after his trusty lieutenant was fast asleep, the expedition's leader lay awake in the gray dawn, criticizing himself.

BR-R-R-RING!

Sitting up at once, Roger reached convulsively for the alarm clock to smother it and turn it off. Thumbs sat up, yawning and stretching.

"Let's go."

They heard stirrings in the next tent, and then sudden action. The zipper snarled open, and Shirley burst outside.

"Roger! We're late!"

Roger stuck his head out of their tent and smiled maliciously. From the viewpoint of a sister, it must have been the nastiest smile imaginable.

"No, we're not. You're late," he said, and told her briefly what had happened. She was satisfactorily furious.

"You let me miss it! That's a dirty trick!"

"There wasn't time to wake you up. It wouldn't have done any good anyway. We were too late."

"Why were you late?"

The question was inevitable, of course; and, to Roger's credit, he was unsparing with himself in explaining. Shirley, needless to say, felt much better.

"You and your old watches!" she jeered.

They crawled out of the tents, straightened their clothing so that it wouldn't look too slept-in, and went to get their bicycles.

"We'll ride in as if we'd just come from home. Let's go."

When the poultry yard came in sight, they found that Dick had not drawn as good an audience as Tom had.

Maybe the novelty was wearing off. At any rate, only Mr. Chadburn and Zoltan were standing around the body this time.

"What? Again?" cried Roger, putting all the surprise he could muster into his voice.

Mr. Chadburn glanced around at him briefly and nodded.

"I'd like to know what's going on around here!" he declared. Hands on hips, he stared down at the latest corpse. "Well, let's get rid of this thing. I don't imagine the Plummingtons would want goose two days in a row —"

"Be nice for Kossuth Club dinner tomorrow," suggested Zoltan. "All right?"

"Sure, sure, give it to your club, but get it out of here before Mrs. Chadburn takes it into her head to come out." (The Lajos Kossuth Hungarian-American Club, which met regularly in the Grange Hall, was the Dubrovnics' principal source of social life.)

They watched Zoltan carry away the goose to wrap it and put it in a sack. Mr. Chadburn was wearing his faded farm clothes, indicative of the fact that he was not going to the city to make another million dollars that day. He rubbed his double-chinned jaw and looked rooster-fierce.

"Beats me why anyone would do such a thing. I suppose I ought to notify the police . . ."

"Constable Stubbert? And have him trampling your flowers?"

Mr. Chadburn grinned dryly.

"You're right. He wouldn't accomplish a thing, except damage. I may have to report it, but I'll try to keep him away. Well, Roger, what do *you* think about this?"

"I don't know, Mr. Chadburn."

"Well, I won't say a certain competitor of mine is behind this, but I wouldn't . . ."

"You mean . . . ?"

"Never mind what I mean. Forget I said it," he snapped, and turned away. Over his shoulder, as he went to the gate, he added, "Eggs will be ready shortly. Zaza's working on them."

This time, apparently, crime was being taken more in stride. It was business as usual.

"Let's go see Old Sarge," Roger suggested casually to his assistants. They followed Mr. Chadburn out of the poultry yard and closed the gate. He went toward the house, and they walked away toward the path to Old Sarge's cottage. Behind them Zoltan came out with Dick neatly shrouded and got into the pickup truck. None too soon, either, because when they looked toward the main house they saw Mrs. Chadburn just coming out.

They examined the path once more. Nosing along beside it in his best bloodhound manner, Roger was soon excited by unmistakably fresh footprints.

"Uncle Willie's again, too, they are!"

The fresh footprints going toward the cottage were occasionally overlapped by footprints coming back. They continued on all the way to the cottage.

Mounting the small front porch Old Sarge himself had added to the otherwise prefabricated house, Roger knocked on the screen door and called.

"Sarge!"

"Who's that? Roger? Come in."

The smell of violently strong coffee was in the air. They entered the compact sitting room, as Old Sarge called it, and their eyes went at once to the Cavalry saber hanging in its metal scabbard on the wall, suspended from a nail by a cord that ran through two eyelets near the top and bottom of the scabbard. Old Sarge appeared with a mug of steaming coffee in his hand.

"Morning, kids. I was just fixing my breakfast. What's up?"

Roger was suddenly all but tongue-tied. The idea of questioning their old friend was distasteful and embarrassing. However, it was one of those things any criminologist had to face once in a while, if he wanted to be a real detective. It was all in a day's work.

"Well, it's about Tom and Dick, Sarge."

Old Sarge looked puzzled.

"What do you mean, Tom and Dick?"

"Well, now that Dick's been killed, too —"

"*What?*"

If Old Sarge's surprise was put on, then he had wasted a lot of time in the Cavalry. He should have been an actor.

"What are you talking about?" he demanded.

"Gosh, didn't you know, Sarge? Somebody killed Dick this morning."

The old man's eyes popped and his mustache twitched. He set his mug of coffee down on a table so hard it slopped over.

"What in the name of — Why didn't somebody —?"

With a vigor that was impressive in one of his years, Old Sarge strode to the door and out, heading toward the scene of the now multiple murders.

"Mr. Chadburn's gone back to the house," Roger called after him, and the old soldier wheeled right, changing direction, without so much as a backward glance.

Nothing could have suited Roger better than to find himself alone in Old Sarge's sitting room under circumstances that made it unnecessary to trespass there. Similar thoughts were in Thumbs's and Shirley's minds. The three of them converged immediately on the saber.

"Don't touch it!" warned Roger. "I want to see something."

Putting his head almost against the wall, he carefully inspected the underside of the cord.

"Ah!" cried Inspector Tearle. Ever so carefully he lifted the cord away from the nail.

"Hah!" cried Inspector Tearle. A worn mark on the underside of the cord showed where it had rested on the nail for a long time — but the mark was half an inch from the place where the cord now crossed the nail. Where the cord now crossed, it was hardly marked.

"Someone," concluded Roger, "has taken this off the wall very recently, and whoever it was didn't hang it back up in quite the same way!"

9

THE AIR crackled with the excitement of discovery.

"What are we going to do now?"

"Wait till Old Sarge comes back," said Roger grimly. "Now we've *got* to see what he has to say about Uncle Willie."

Shirley fidgeted over to the door and glared out.

"We can't just stand around waiting!"

"Yes, we can. He won't be long. He'll come back to finish his breakfast. We've got to talk to him in private, and this is the place to do it, right where the saber is."

The burdens of leadership can be heavy. George Washington knew it. King Arthur knew it. Alexander the Great knew it. And now Inspector Tearle knew it. A leader was constantly having to set an example for his followers. At a time when simply standing and waiting made him so nervous he was ready to crawl up the wall, the leader had nevertheless to simply stand and wait. So he did. Shirley sat down, sprang up, sat down, sprang up, groaned, glared out the door again, and sat down again. Thumbs passed the time as best he could by picking at a scab on his elbow.

Finally, the sound of footsteps took them all to the door. Old Sarge was returning.

"Durn fool business! Craziest thing I ever heerd of," he was muttering. He stopped when he saw them waiting, and stared through the screen. "You still here?"

"We wanted to talk to you a minute, Sarge."

"Oh. Did, hey?"

He came inside. Roger's heart skipped a beat, because the old soldier's air was suddenly furtive. No question about it. Definitely furtive.

"What's on your mind?"

Roger braced himself and began.

"It's about Uncle Willie, Sarge . . ."

The ancient blue eyes were startled. Undeniably startled.

"What about him?"

"He was here on the farm the night Tom was killed."

Old Sarge looked torn. Torn between a tendency to admire Inspector Tearle and a desire to wring his neck.

"How did you know that?" he growled.

Roger caught his breath. It was true! But now he had to be careful, because he couldn't give Miss Grimshaw away.

"I've been putting two and two together," he replied vaguely. "Footprints, and stuff . . ."

Still staring at him, Old Sarge shook his head. Then he sat down on the sagging sofa, picked up his mug of coffee, and took a pull at it.

"Phoo! Cold." He held out the mug to Shirley. "Dump this out, Shirl, and pour me some fresh from the pot. On the double!"

She hurried into the kitchen. Old Sarge turned to Roger again.

"Well, you're right, Willie *was* over here that night, but it warn't the way you're thinking." He folded his arms and crossed his legs like a man settling back to tell a story. "What happened was this. Long about two o'clock in the morning Willie woke up with a terrible toothache."

"Oh?" Roger remembered how Uncle Willie had looked as they rode by the night before. Sitting on the porch looking glum, with his jaw in his hand. "Has he still got the toothache?"

Old Sarge nodded.

"It's kept nagging at him, and so has that wife of his. She finally nagged him into making an appointment with Doc Kepnikoff over in Gainesville for later on this morning. So anyways, that night Willie stood it for a while, but he was wishing like all git-out he could take a little drink of something to ease the pain, or anyway help him forget it. But Mabel, she won't let him keep a drop in the house. She can smell it out no matter where he hides it. He gave up on that years ago. But he knew I always keep something around, and finally it was hurting him so bad he decided to git up and sneak out of the house and come over here."

Roger nodded understandingly. Rumor had it that whenever the two old cronies got together at Old Sarge's cottage for a game of cribbage, it was their custom to take a little something to protect them from the damp night air.

"Luckily Willie and Mabel sleep in separate rooms, because each one says the other'n snores like a pig, so Willie was able to sneak out all right. He was footing it along the path and was nearly here when all at once he heerd some peculiar noises coming from the direction of the henhouse. It was just commencing to git light enough so's he could see the path a few feet ahead of him, and the fowls had come out, and them geese was sounding off as usual, and Willie was swearing at them under his breath as he walked along, when he heerd this noise. It was as if one of them let loose with a goose-yell, he says. It was such a curious sound that Willie stopped to listen, and then climbed the bank, figgering to have a look."

Old Sarge paused to take a pull at the fresh mug of coffee Shirley had brought him.

"Ah! That's better."

Now that he was into his yarn, it was obvious he was

enjoying telling it and wanted to wring the full dramatic effects out of it. Saucer-eyed, Shirley asked, "What did he see, Sarge?"

"Well, sir, I wish I knew. Iff'n he did see anything at all, that is. You know Willie's sight ain't too good any more. He has to squint at things purty close, leastways in a bad light. But he swears he warn't more'n halfway to the henhouse when he liked to jumped out of his skin."

Again Old Sarge paused for refreshment, smacked his lips, enjoyed his young friends' suffering, and finally relieved it.

"He swears that just then something went by him like greased lightning. Something black."

His listeners awarded this statement the gasp it so richly deserved.

"Golly! What was it, Sarge?"

"I already told you, I wish I knew. Hard to be sure it was *anything*. I can tell you one thing for sure — when you're nerved up in uncertain light, it's not hard to see all kinds of things, specially black ones. But anyways, Willie claims that *something* went by him almost close enough to touch, if he'd been inclined to, which he wasn't."

"What kind of noise did the thing make?"

"That's the funny part of it, too. Willie says he can't recall it made any sound at all. In fact, that was one of the parts that scared him the most, he says."

Roger and his assistants exchanged wildly speculative

glances. Something black! Black and silent! The mystery had suddenly deepened beyond all comprehension, if Uncle Willie could be believed.

"Well, for a while Willie just stood there petrified. He says he hadn't felt that way since the day he almost walked into an open elevator shaft back in 1922. After a time, though, he got back the use of his limbs, and when he did he walked on over to the henhouse, where the queer noises had come from. And there was Tom, lying in the yard, with his head chopped off."

Roger's imagination was powerfully at work. He could

see it all as if he had been there. Uncle Willie in his baggy old coat, in the dim morning light, gaping through the fence at the corpse in the poultry yard . . .

Old Sarge chuckled.

"Nothing like a good scare to cure a toothache, for the time being, at least. Willie forgot all about his tooth. When he saw Tom lying there, all he could think about was hightailing off the farm as fast as he could git. After all the talking he'd done about them geese, he knew it would look mighty suspicious if anybody found out he was around when a thing like that happened. So he took off for home by a roundabout way, sneaked in without waking up Mabel, and that was that."

With a couple of powerful gulps that sent his Adam's apple bouncing up and down like a pingpong ball shooting the rapids, Old Sarge drained his coffee mug and set it aside.

"Now, you mustn't say a word about this to anyone, because there ain't no point in getting Willie into trouble with young Chadburn — or with Mabel, neither."

"We won't say anything," promised Roger. He could not, however, help thinking that what with Miss Grimshaw still to be reckoned with, Uncle Willie might not have heard the last of his escapade. But that was Uncle Willie's problem. "Well, that's some story, Sarge. What do you make of it?"

"Beats me. I can't think of any kind of black Thing it might have been. I'm inclined to figger the dark was playing tricks on Willie. I just don't know what else to think."

Regrettable possibilities were passing through Roger's mind. Old Sarge, after all, was a great hand with a tall tale. The whole story could be made up out of whole cloth, to cover up for his crony. If it were, there was a way to find out.

"When did Uncle Willie tell you all this, Sarge? Was it yesterday morning at the post office, when you went for the mail?"

"No, I didn't see him then. Willie come over here last night, about nine o'clock, to get something for his tooth, because it was nagging him again."

A smile relieved Roger's sad-eyed face. The fresh footprints on the path were satisfactorily explained. Now it was time to take Old Sarge into their confidence. Roger walked over to the saber.

"Here's one reason we wondered about Uncle Willie, Sarge."

The old Cavalryman twisted around in his chair to send a puzzled glance up at his prize possession.

"What about it?"

"When did you last take it off the wall?"

"Hey? Well, let me see . . . Been quite a spell now. Not since last fall, I'd say. Every so often I wipe it off good and put on a new light coat of oil, but it don't need too much attention. I strung a new cord onto it to hang it up by — old one was getting shabby-looking —"

"Good! That really proves it!"

"Proves what?"

Roger pointed to the place on the underside of the cord.

"If the cord is new, that makes it all the more certain. You can see a deep mark in the cord that shows where it rested on the nail — but the mark's not lined up with the nail now."

"It ain't?" Old Sarge got to his feet and peered closely. "Well, I swan! You're right. That there saber's been moved!"

"Uncle Willie ever take it down to look at it?"

"Willie? Why, sure."

"When?" cried Roger.

" 'Bout ten years ago, I'd say, first time he come over."

"Oh."

Old Sarge's face underwent a comical transformation as he suddenly realized which way the wind was blowing.

"Wait a gol-durned minute here! Is that what you're gitting at? You think . . . ?"

"Yes, Sarge. It could have been the murder weapon."

The old man looked almost insulted.

"Ah, come on, now!"

"But it could, Sarge. Those heads weren't chopped off, they were lopped off."

"Lopped off?"

"Yes, sir. Lopped off. There wasn't a chop mark on

the ground anywhere, either time, that I could find. I don't think the killer used a hatchet or an axe. I think he used something he could swing, like a sword or . . . a saber."

With his long jaw flapped apart beneath his straggly gray mustache, Old Sarge stared first at the weapon and then at Roger and then at the weapon again.

"Well, I'll be . . . !"

Lifting the cord off the nail, Old Sarge grasped the scabbard and pulled the blade free. He had shown it to them before, a couple of years ago, but now it looked twice as dangerous as it had then. Now it gleamed wickedly in a shaft of sunlight that angled through an east window. The old warrior examined it closely. He ran the sides of the blade between thumb and forefinger, then rubbed his fingertips together.

"Not much oil left on her, but she's clean as a whistle."

"Someone *could* have used her, though, and wiped her clean afterwards. Someone could have snuck in here in the middle of the night, borrowed her, and brought her back afterwards. If that black Thing Uncle Willie thought he saw really was something, it could have been somebody bringing her back."

Old Sarge thought about it for a moment, his weather-beaten face screwed up agonizingly. Then he snorted like Thunderbolt.

"It's too much to believe! I'm not a light sleeper, I'll

admit, but for someone to come tramping in here —"

"Someone might have come in very quietly, Sarge."

"Hmp! Even so, it's more'n I can swallow."

Nevertheless, for a moment he stared irresolutely at the saber. "Course, I could hide it now, just in case somebody has got funny ideas about Harry, too."

"No, don't do that, Sarge," said Roger quickly. "We'll never catch the killer that way. Besides, it wouldn't protect Harry. If the killer couldn't find your saber, he'd use something else."

"Hmm. I reckon you're right." Still staring at it, Old Sarge returned the saber to its place on the wall. Then he turned back to them. "Well, I got to get my breakfast et."

"And we've got to deliver our eggs. See you later, Sarge."

As they started to leave, the reflective look on his wrinkled old face became quizzical, and a raffish twinkle brightened his eyes.

"So Dick finally got what was coming to him, did he? Can't say as I'm sorry, after what he done to me."

He cocked his head challengingly at Roger.

"For that matter, how do you know I didn't kill him myself?"

Halfway out the door, Roger turned, grinning every bit as wickedly as the old man.

"You couldn't have, Sarge. You're too tall," he said, and left their friend with his mouth ajar.

As they walked back along the path, Roger was deep in thought.

"Hey, Roger, do you think Uncle Willie really saw a black Thing?" asked Thumbs.

Roger shook his head.

"If he saw something black it wasn't a Thing. A Thing wouldn't bring along a box to stand on."

The excitement of the chase was gripping Roger more strongly than ever now.

"All I know is, we'd better be in our tents tonight, and this time we'll be awake and ready when the time comes."

He stopped and faced them dramatically.

"I'll tell you one thing. I wouldn't want to be in Harry's shoes for anything in the world!"

Naturally Shirley took it upon herself to point out that geese don't wear shoes. It was just the sort of thing a sister would do.

"Well, you know what I mean," snapped Roger. "I think he's a gone goose, if ever there was one!"

"You mean . . . ?"

"Yes. The murderer is bound to strike again!"

Little did Inspector Tearle know that before any murderer could strike, disaster would strike him first, at home.

10

Soon after they had returned to the murder scene, which Roger wanted to examine again, the pickup truck came rattling into sight from the back road. Zoltan stopped at the utility barn and went inside. In a moment he reappeared and came muttering toward them to say the eggs were ready.

For the next hour or so they were occupied with commercial matters. They stopped at home for a quick breakfast, after which Shirley ate her way around their route as usual, picking up a cookie here and a cupcake there whenever they were offered.

It was when they had delivered the last of their eggs at the end of their route and were cycling toward home that Amos Chilton and his wife went by in their station wagon, reminding Roger once again of the still unsolved Chilton Watch Case. Mrs. Chilton was at the wheel, probably taking her husband to his shop so that she could have the car.

Roger waved as they went by, and then several notions clicked together in his head like billiard balls. Skidding his bike to a side-slip stop, he motioned to his assistants.

"Quick, follow that car!" he cried, unable as usual to resist a touch of the theatrical when the chase was on.

There was no time for the others to ask questions, and no need to, since it was obvious that if they turned around and raced after Roger as he raced after the car, they would know soon enough what was going on.

Mrs. Chilton drove with the brisk assurance of one traveling a route she had driven a thousand times. They

were not able to keep up with her. By the time they came within sight of the print shop, Mr. Chilton had gone inside and she was pulling away.

"Come on!" Roger ordered, beckoning over his shoulder. "Maybe she'll stop somewhere."

She did, on the other side of the square. She was standing beside her car, talking to a friend, when Roger and his assistants arrived.

"Mrs. Chilton!"

She glanced around.

"Why, hello, Inspector. What's up?"

Two minutes later the station wagon was heading back toward the print shop behind a bicycle escort. Arriving at the shop, they all went inside, including Mrs. Chilton's friend, who had come along.

Amos Chilton was standing at a type case, hand-setting type. His head bobbed up in surprise as the three youngsters and two women planted themselves in a semicircle in front of him. Mrs. Chilton eyed her husband with sharp pleasure.

"All right, Inspector, tell him, just the way you told me."

"Yes, ma'am. Mr. Chilton, do you know much about magic?"

"Magic? No. What about it?"

"Well, the secret of a magician's tricks is distraction. At just the right instant, he distracts the attention of his audience, so that they're always looking at the wrong place, and don't see him do his sleight-of-hand."

"Do tell," said Mr. Chilton dryly. "What's this all about?"

"When you drove by us a few minutes ago, I suddenly thought of what might have happened to your watch."

"Did? And what was that?"

"Well, when you went to the Bilsop wedding, you were late. I figured Mrs. Chilton probably had the car ready, waiting for you. That meant she was driving and you got in on the passenger side."

Amos Chilton's head bobbed again.

"Matter of fact, that's true."

"She was jawing at you for being late, you said, and she says you were jawing right back. And that's where your magic door handle came in."

"My what?"

"I remembered once when my father caught his coat-sleeve on a car door handle. I thought maybe since you wear your watch on your right wrist, it might have caught on the door handle. What with that pin in the strap that wasn't holding right, the handle could have picked your watch off your wrist without your ever knowing it, while your attention was somewhere else, jawing at Mrs. Chilton. Then it could have fallen down and slid under the car seat, and . . ."

Roger made a pass in the air above his head. He was

a pretty fair magician himself. It looked as if he had plucked something shiny out of thin air. A wristwatch, with a band that had come loose at one end. With a sheepish grin that made fun of his own showmanship, Roger handed the watch to its astonished owner.

"Well, I'll be everlastingly . . . I could have sworn on a stack of Bibles I never put that watch back on my wrist!"

Amos Chilton put down the stick of type he was working on, and laid his hand on Roger's shoulder. "Inspector, do you still want to learn how to set type?"

"I sure do!"

"Then you be here at four o'clock this afternoon for your first lesson, and that's a date! But by George, I could have *sworn* I never put that watch back on . . ."

Flushed with triumph, Roger pedaled home again, trailed by his admiring assistants. Even Shirley had to admit he had closed the Chilton Watch Case in high style. He burst into the house eager to tell his mother all about it, but she got in her news first.

"Well! I'm glad you two are home," she declared, beaming at them. "I've got a wonderful surprise for you."

"You have?" Shirley's mouth was already watering. "Did you make a chocolate cake? Or apple pie? What, Mom?"

Their mother laughed.

"No, it's nothing to eat. It's better than that," she said, while Shirley looked amazed and tried to think of something better than food. "Your grandfather just telephoned, and guess what? He and Grandma are going to get away a week early on their trip to Europe! They're flying from Kennedy International Airport in New York tomorrow morning — and we're going to drive there this afternoon so as to be on hand to see them off!"

Shirley automatically cheered, because she loved trips. Ordinarily Roger loved them, too, but on this occasion he was stunned.

"You mean we're going to be gone *overnight?*"

"Well, of course, silly. We're going to stay in a motel tonight right at the airport. Won't that be fun?"

If Sherlock Holmes, just as he was closing in on his arch-enemy, Professor Moriarty, had been told he had to drop everything to run over to Buckingham Palace for dinner with Queen Victoria, he could not have greeted the news with more mixed emotions.

"But we can't go away *now*, Mom! We've got to be in our tents again tonight for sure!"

His mother's mouth began to look firm. She could hardly be blamed, of course. It was exasperating to have her nice exciting news get such a poor reception.

"Roger, I'm surprised at you. Your grandparents are certainly a lot more important than a couple of dead geese. Besides, even if you were going to be here tonight

I wouldn't *dream* of letting you camp out and get up in the middle of the night again. Look at those circles under your eyes!"

"Aw, I feel fine, Mom!"

"You don't look it."

"Well, I sure won't get much sleep in any crumby old motel at Kennedy Airport!" grumbled Roger.

"Oh, yes, you will." Her foot was beginning to tap out a message, which she proceeded to put into words. "Now, make up your mind to it, Roger Tearle. We're going to leave here right after lunch. I'm not going to have your grandfather and grandmother go off on a long trip to Europe without seeing you, and you know very well you wouldn't want them to, either, if you'd stop and think about it."

Roger wriggled miserably on the horns of his dilemma. It was true, of course, he *wouldn't* want them to. He was fond of his grandparents. They were fun to be with. They gave him wonderful presents, and generally acted the way grandparents should. But why did they have to pick *now*, of all times?

As Mr. Shakespeare's King Macbeth pointed out at a time during which things were not going altogether well for *him*, "When sorrows come, they come not single spies, but in battalions." Roger became aware of still another sorrow on his list.

"Oh, gosh! And now I won't even be here for my first

type-setting lesson from Mr. Chilton — and by the time we get back he'll be too busy again and will keep putting it off, same as before!"

He flung himself into a chair, all but tearful with frustration.

"It's not fair!"

"Now, Roger —"

"But anyway, that's still not the big thing. The big thing is still my murder case," he said desperately, "and everything's liable to come to a head tonight!"

"Harry's head!" cried Shirley, and of course she thought she was awfully funny. Their mother laughed. Even Thumbs laughed, the traitor! Inspector Tearle's world lay in ruins. The murderer had a clear field now. All he had to do was stroll over to the poultry yard by dawn's early light next morning, wait for Harry to appear, and take care of his unfinished business. No one would be the wiser. Inspector Tearle would be many miles away, trying to get some sleep in a crumby old motel at Kennedy International Airport.

Roger was glum as the family station wagon traveled smoothly along the superhighway toward New York City. As a rule he would have admired the performance of its powerful eight-cylinder engine, which he understood intimately, but today he was in no mood for mechanics. Behind him, back at the scene, was left only Thumbs Thorndyke. It was as if Sherlock Holmes, off to see the

Queen, were forced to pin all his hopes on the bumbling efforts of his friend Doctor Watson. Roger did not know which would be worse — to have Thumbs bungle the case in his absence, or solve it.

Not that Thumbs was likely to do either, because he had admitted he was not about to spend a night alone in their tent in the hollow. He summed it up very simply.

"I'd be scared out of my britches," he said, using an old-fashioned expression they had picked up from Old Sarge.

During the ride Roger did a good deal of thinking on the subject of grandparents. They were necessary, of course. You couldn't very well have a family without them. But *why* did they have to do things like flying to Europe a week early, when by next week he could probably have had his murder case all cleared up and been ready to enjoy every detail of seeing them off? It certainly wasn't fair. There wasn't anything fair about it.

He received only a limited amount of sympathy from his parents. At first they tried to mollify him by complimenting him on his brilliant handling of the Chilton Watch Case. But then they turned on him. They told him to get that abused look off his face. By the time they reached the airport, Roger had been given a couple of pretty severe talkings-to. He had even been threatened with bodily harm by his father. Well, plenty of detectives, especially private eyes, had to put up with some pushing around and leaning on. It was all part of the game. But why take punishment when it wasn't in line of duty and wouldn't advance your case any? In time — just in time — Roger decided he had better stop pulling a long face about things and be a bit more cheerful.

His grandparents' pleasure when they saw him, and the excitement they displayed about their trip, made him partly forget his troubles. At least it made him remember how fond he was of them. They all had a good dinner together, and presently it was bedtime. Though he had resigned himself to tossing and turning all night, he almost suspected his mother of having slipped a sleeping pill into his milk at dinner, because he could not hold his eyes open. The next thing he knew it was early morning and time to get up and see the plane leave.

Roger stared out at the gray morning light, and his powerful imagination went to work. He was back on Hessian Run Farm, creeping along the side of the utility barn to peep around the corner through the tall grass and watch for Something Black to appear silently beside the fence of the poultry yard . . . Something black . . . He had fallen asleep thinking about that black something, and now it was in the forefront of his thoughts again. What was it he had once read concerning something black? The question had been in the back of his mind ever since Old Sarge had told them about Uncle Willie's experience. Something black . . .

There were thousands of things that were black. But what was it he had once read about that might fit into . . . ?

007!

All at once he remembered an exploit of the famous Secret Agent 007, and his hair stood on end. Great detectives have one thing in common. They are always likely to have sudden flashes of intuition, wherein all at once a whole train of possibilities becomes crystal-clear. And that was what had happened to Inspector Tearle. His solution of the Chilton Watch Case had been a minor example of such a flash. But this was a major one. This was a bolt of lightning.

And it was just as shattering. Because now, in an instant, he could see how everything *might* have been done, and why. He could see it, and yet there was nothing he could do about it because he was far from the scene of the crime. Indeed, the final crime had undoubtedly even now — already! — been committed!

11

ROGER faced their return home, late that afternoon, with a combination of eagerness and dread. In short, he could hardly wait to find out what he didn't want to know.

"I wonder how Thumbs managed, delivering the eggs all by himself?" said Shirley, as the car neared East Widmarsh. "It must have been a lot of work. I'll bet he had to make three trips."

"I just hope he didn't break any eggs. Soon as we get home I'm going to call him up."

"What will you do if he says Harry got killed last night?"

"I don't know," said Roger, and glowered moodily out the window.

"Go on. Call him up and get it over with," said his mother, when the car had turned into the drive and stopped. Roger walked into the house as deliberately as he could — he was determined to walk, not run. He dialed the Thorndykes' number.

He waited.

No answer.

He hung up and went outside to help bring in the bags.

"Well?" asked his father.

Roger's tight smile was the badge of a martyr.

"Wouldn't you know it? He's not even home."

His father eyed him, and shook his head.

"Get on your bike and ride out to the farm and see for yourself," he ordered. "I can't stand the sight of you much longer."

"Okay, Dad."

"I'll go too," said Shirley, but her father had an order for her as well.

"No, you stay here. Let him suffer alone," he said, and received a grateful look from his son for such understanding.

Alone, then, Inspector Tearle set out on his bitter trail down the shady street and across the open meadow toward the farmyard. With heavy heart, and head bowed over handlebars, he pumped toward the scene.

He was halfway across the meadow when a sound made his head come up. Even the notes of the distant trumpet in Beethoven's opera *Fidelio*, which his grandmother had once taken him to see in New York, were no more

thrilling a lifesaver than was the sound that came racket-
ing down the wind now to make him pedal madly forward. Like a two-wheeled streak Roger blurred between
the barns and into the farmyard and came to a stop that
nearly disabled him.

There, honking noisily in the center of the poultry
yard, stood Harry, triumphantly alive, and looking as
mean as ever.

It was a new Inspector Tearle who re-crossed the meadow, a blithe and debonair Inspector who was singing loudly in a voice not much better than Harry's, for music was not one of Roger's major talents. But no matter. All was right with the world again, and more than right. If his theories were correct, his first murder case would be solved by morning.

Because the murderer would have to strike tonight, or not at all!

It was a fine clear night, there was no fog in the hollow, and Roger was so pleased to be back that he had even allowed Shirley to stick her head in their tent again until it was time to go to sleep.

Not that it had been easy to reach their objective. Their mother had not been disposed to allow them another camp-out, for the reasons she had mentioned earlier. Only because Roger had assured her this would be the last time, and he would never ask again, had she finally given in.

"I don't see how you could be so sure this would be the night," said Shirley, in between bites. She was eating an after-dinner snack, half a dozen ginger snaps.

"If my theory is right, this *has* to be the night," said Roger. "I wish I could explain everything to you, but if I'm wrong I'd rather that nobody, not even you and Thumbs, ever knew what my idea was. It would be so terrible, if I'm wrong. You'll understand when the time comes."

"Well, okay," sighed Shirley, and solaced herself with another cookie.

For a while the crackle of ginger snaps was the only sound in the tent. Then Thumbs had a question.

"And you mean we won't even have to stand watches this time?"

"That's right. We can use your alarm clock. It's better to wake up early than to stand watches. If we set it half an hour early there won't be any danger of the murderer hearing it, because he probably won't be around yet, and at any rate he won't be near here."

"Gosh!"

"Of course, we won't take any extra chances. I'll have the alarm set for 'Soft,' and keep it inside my sleeping bag, and I'll muffle it as much as I can."

"WHO-O-O-O?"

This time the hoot of the resident owl hardly made them jump. Well, it made them jump a little, but not nearly as much as two nights earlier. This time Inspector Tearle merely smiled.

"Who?" he murmured. "That's what we'll find out — tomorrow morning!"

BRI-R-R-ING!

Roger's eyes popped open and he made a grab for the

clock. In the darkness his fingers found the button and stifled the alarm. Instantly his heart was beating fast.

The great moment had come! He poked Thumbs awake and slipped out into the dark to wake Shirley.

The night had been clear and cool, and such a night is never colder and darker than just before the first signs of dawn appear. They had slept in their clothes, so there was no time wasted in dressing. They were soon outside in the pit blackness of the hollow, unable to see each other even at close range. Shirley and Thumbs followed Roger by sound, rather than sight, as he felt his way from tree to tree and up the side of the hollow. Shirley, bringing up the rear, had it the easiest, because she had the chunk-chunk sound of Thumbs's head bouncing from low-hanging branch to branch to go by. Their teeth chattered as frigid air seemed to bite through drowsy flesh and into the very marrow of their bones before the blood had a chance to start stirring through their veins.

When they reached the level of the road, they could make out shadowy forms and distances. Above them the sky was a twinkling showcase with a milkcan-full of diamonds thrown across it. They could see the road ahead of them, a pale buff ribbon winding between two hulking black masses that were the barns. Silently Roger led the way toward a stand of tall grass between the road and the utility barn. There they went down on their bellies. Dropping into the icy dew was like plunging into a cold shower. Carefully they inched forward until they could see the poultry yard.

All was still, with that breathless stillness of the last moments of night. Nothing stirred anywhere. Caught by the wonder of it, they were silent and awed, and almost forgot what they were waiting for. Then, bit by bit, blacks became dark grays. Their eyes sought the black square low in the gray side of the henhouse, the square they knew was the door. How soon would it open, and what would happen then?

A sound. It was rolling up! Cackles and clucks, then indignant squawks and a bullying honk. Harry! Harry, pushing the chickens aside, was on his way out!

Dimly, but unmistakably, a white form began to move across the poultry yard. A head could be seen on the end of its long neck, pecking the ground at each waddling step. On across the yard went the big goose, peck by peck. Though his heart was in his throat, Roger managed to smile to himself. A trail of corn? Had a trail of corn been laid across the yard in the night? Whatever it was, Harry was advancing nearer and nearer the right side of the fence. Now he was quite near . . .

Not even Roger's preconceived theory, assisted by his powerful imagination, had been enough to prepare him for what happened next.

Outside the fence, a black shape seemed to rise up out of the ground. Startled, Harry looked up and honked in

123

alarm. A gray glint of cold steel flashed in the air, the honk ended abruptly, and the black form melted into the earth again.

Roger opened his numb lips to whisper, "Follow me!" But though his lips seemed to move, and form the words, no sound came forth. His vocal cords might have suffered the same fate as Harry's, for all the use he could make of them.

He gulped, and by the time he was ready to try again, he thought better of it. Sooner or later the moment always comes when the master detective has to go it alone. For Inspector Tearle, that moment was now. Shirley, and particularly Thumbs, blundering along behind him in the darkness would make so much noise that all might be lost. Roger knew where he wanted to go, and he had a chance of going there silently and undetected — if he went alone.

"Stay here and keep watch!" he whispered to the others, and quietly got to his feet. For once, neither of them said, "I want to go along!" Somewhere in the darkness ahead was a frightful black shape with a saber, and that black shape had scared them speechless and stiff.

With only his triphammer heart to keep him company, Roger picked his way along the path toward Old Sarge's cottage. A dozen times black shapes sprang at him from the sides of the path, only to become trees or bushes after he was half dead from fright.

When he had nearly reached the cottage, he froze in his tracks to listen. He heard nothing. But then, as he crouched in the path, a rustle seemed to cross the grass in front of the cottage and a black blot to darken the deep gray of fading night under the trees. Then all was still again.

Somehow Roger found the courage to creep forward and keep going, toward the Chadburn house now. And he was in time for the sort of sound he had hoped to hear.

The click of a door latch. Someone had quietly closed the kitchen door.

If nothing can be more frightening than darkness, nothing can be more startling than light. Light suddenly fringed the kitchen window blinds. Tiptoeing forward, Roger peered in around a corner of one blind that did not quite cover a window.

What he saw was enough. All he needed.

Stepping to the door, Inspector Tearle drew in a big shaky breath, and then rapped once, twice, thrice.

12

EXCLAMATIONS. Consternation.

"What the devil . . . ?"

Scurrying sounds. Then slippered footsteps coming toward the door, and the gruff voice of Mr. Chadburn.

"Who's there?"

"It's Roger, sir."

"*Roger?* Well, for . . . !"

The door opened. Roger blinked, half-blinded in the sudden rectangle of light. Mr. Chadburn, in pajamas, bathrobe, and slippers, squinted out at him.

"Roger! What the devil are you doing prowling around at this hour?"

"May I come in and tell you, sir?"

Mr. Chadburn jerked his head sideways.

"Why, sure, come in. I couldn't sleep, so I was sitting here in the kitchen having a cup of coffee." He sat down again, picked up his cup, and drank, looking narrowly at

Roger over the rim. "What's up, boy? Sit down, sit down."

Roger perched on the edge of a kitchen chair opposite him, across the table, under a central light.

"Harry's just been killed, Mr. Chadburn."

The millionaire financier and chicken-fancier lowered his cup.

"What?"

"We were keeping watch, and we saw it happen."

Mr. Chadburn's astonishment was unquestionably genuine.

"By George! Did you see who did it?"

"Yes, sir."

"Who?"

"Someone dressed all in black."

Mr. Chadburn stared at him for a long moment. Then he sat back in his chair.

"Well, I'll be a son of a gun." He turned and called over his shoulder. "Kiddo! Kiddo, will you come give me some more coffee, and get something for Roger here?"

From his room off the kitchen, Kiddo Nockamura appeared in a Japanese kimono.

"Yes, Mr. Chadburn." He beamed and bowed at Roger. "You rike grassa mirk and mebbe nice piece of chock-rat cake à ra Nockamura I make rast night?"

"Yes, thanks," said Roger, who was used to Kiddo's Japanese-style difficulty with the letter "*l.*" For an instant he was almost sorry Shirley was not present. She would have swooned with delight. Chocolate cake à la Nockamura (with slivered almonds on top, and certain secret touches that were the despair of all East Widmarsh housewives who had ever tasted it) was famous for miles around.

"Now, then. This something in black," said Mr. Chadburn, plucking at his lips. "I wonder who it could have been? I tell you, I'll bet that scoundrel Gilhuly would know. This sounds professional. I'll bet he's behind it all."

"I think I know how it was done, sir," said Roger.

Deftly Kiddo set a plate in front of him with a towering piece of chocolate cake on it, and put a glass of Hessian Run Farm milk beside it.

"Thanks, Kiddo. Well, this man was all dressed in black, and he killed Harry by standing on a box outside the fence and lopping his head off with a saber."

"A saber? Of all the crazy things!"

"Yes, sir."

"Why on earth would anybody do a thing like that?"

"That's the part I think I know, Mr. Chadburn. I had to go to New York with my family Tuesday, and while we were away I remembered something I read once in a book."

Prudently, and quite sensibly, Roger paused to take a bite of cake. Might as well have some while he could. He tasted it, and even in his present tense frame of mind he was enraptured by it. Shirley would have been in seventh heaven.

"What was it you read, Roger?" asked Mr. Chadburn, his fingers drumming lightly on the table. Roger swallowed his bite of cake and took a gulp of milk. His heart was beating hard, and he could not have denied he was scared.

"It was about a special kind of secret Japanese training called the dreaded art of *ninjutsu*," he said — and went straight up in his chair as, behind him, a dish crashed on the floor.

"*Shimatta!*" exclaimed Kiddo, and stooped to pick up the pieces.

Roger got his breath back and plunged ahead.

"The book told about *shimatta*, too," he said. "*Shimatta* is a Japanese exclamation, but not a swearword, because they don't have any swearwords. It's like, 'Oh, darn it!' It means, 'I made a mistake!' "

"I see. Go on," said Mr. Chadburn steadily. "What's this dreaded art called, again?"

"*Ninjutsu*. It's the art of stealth or invisibility. The *ninja* dress in black robes, with a black hood and just slits for their eyes. They can climb any wall, and even walk across ceilings, with special equipment they have. All *ninja* have to graduate in at least ten of the eighteen martial arts of *bushido*, or 'ways of the warrior,' before they can learn to be *ninja*, or 'stealers-in,' " said Roger, quoting from memory now, because he had carefully reread the significant parts of the book since returning home. "The secrets of *ninjutsu* are still closely guarded today and are the property of two main schools, the Iga and the Togakure."

"007," said Mr. Chadburn, nodding, for he was something of a spy story addict himself. He gazed at Roger disapprovingly. "Ian Fleming's James Bond stories are hardly the proper sort of reading for a boy your age."

"I'm only interested in his *detective* methods, sir," replied Roger.

"Mr. Ian Freming," growled Kiddo bitterly. "He talk too much!"

Mr. Chadburn was staring at Kiddo coldly over Roger's

head. Now the millionaire goosebreeder sprang to his feet like a fighting cock.

"Kiddo! How could you do such a thing? If you had to play games, if you wanted to be one of those *ninja* fellows, why did you have to practice on my prize geese? Why did you pick the very week before I was going to register them at the Gaines County poultry show? The very night before, in Harry's case? Now I haven't a single goose left to show, and my bet with Gilhuly will have to be called off. This is too much for me! Go to your room. We'll settle this matter tomorrow!"

Kiddo hissed, Japanese style, and bowed deeply.

"So sorrow," he apologized, bowing again and again, "so sorrow."

"You'll be sorry all right, before I'm through with you," Mr. Chadburn assured him grimly. "I'll see you first thing in the morning."

But before Kiddo could withdraw, Roger had prepared himself to go on.

"But, Mr. Chadburn," he said, "Kiddo didn't do it just for *ninjutsu* practice."

Mr. Chadburn glared down at him.

"He didn't?"

"No, sir. He did it for someone else."

"He — *what?*"

"Yes, sir."

"Roger! Are you suggesting he was in Gilhuly's pay?"

"No, sir."

"Then . . . then . . ."

"What I think, sir, is that something was wrong with Tom, Dick, and Harry, and they had to be got rid of before the poultry show."

Once upon a time Roger had owned a huge red plastic balloon that had been a lot of fun. Then one day it sprang a leak. It didn't pop, the way ordinary rubber balloons do. Instead, it slowly collapsed and sank to the ground, much in the same way Mr. Chadburn now sank into his chair. Roger sat and stared at his cake. After a moment, Mr. Chadburn chuckled philosophically.

"Roger, I've said it before, and I'll say it again. You're the real thing. You're nobody to cross swords with — or sabers, I should say."

He shrugged, and laid his plump hands flat on the table.

"You're right, my boy. You're right. Those geese had developed a rare condition known as Buckmaster's Disease, or Wrinkle Foot. Nobody who didn't know geese would ever have spotted it in its early stages, but those hawk-eyed judges they have over at the poultry show would have. But that's not all. Meantime, Gilhuly has pulled a switch on me. He's substituted some absolutely championship stock he located in Holland for the geese he actually raised himself. He had the new geese flown in secretly. I know this for a fact, but he's covered his tracks so well I could never prove it. Well, could I let him beat me with a bunch of ringers, even if my geese *hadn't* picked up Wrinkle Foot? I had to do something. So I asked Kiddo to do me a favor."

He glanced at Kiddo with a quizzical smile.

"It was an opportunity he'd been waiting for for years. A chance to practice his *ninjutsu*. He's been so happy here in America he hasn't felt like using it on people, so he's felt sort of frustrated."

Mr. Chadburn paused for a melancholy sip of coffee, and then continued. In Roger he had a rapt audience.

"Actually, it was fine, because there wasn't any other way to kill them that wouldn't have looked suspicious. Poisoned grain? How could they eat poisoned grain without half my best chickens eating it, too? It would look mighty strange if three geese toppled over dead in a yard full of healthy chickens, now wouldn't it? So Kiddo looked like the perfect answer."

He shook his head sorrowfully.

"Nothing worked out quite right, though. Kiddo was supposed to finish them all off at once, but the first time he'd only taken care of Tom when some sounds from over Sarge's way scared him off."

Uncle Willie, thought Roger.

"The next time, he fell off his box and made a racket after swinging on Dick. So we skipped a night, to be on the safe side — we *thought*. Of course, that was our big mistake. We passed up the night when you were gone."

Again Mr. Chadburn paused. This time he leaned on the table heavily with his forearms in front of him, cradling his coffee. Then he tipped his head up at Roger with a rueful smile, and once more he shrugged.

"Well, this is the end of the line, Inspector. Naturally, when word of this gets out, we'll have to move away. God knows what Gilhuly will do with this. He'll blow it up all over town and from one end of Wall Street to the other. There won't be anywhere I'll be able to show my face. In fact, I'll be lucky if Mrs. Chadburn doesn't walk out on me, for that matter. You know how she feels about dumb animals, even geese. But don't you worry, Roger. Maybe whoever buys the place will want to keep on raising chickens, same as ever, and I'll certainly recommend you for their egg salesman. Actually, the thing I hate most is the thought of a rat like Gilhuly getting away with mur —"

The word stopped him. He cast a sheepish glance at Roger.

"Well, I guess I shouldn't talk about murder, but you know what I mean."

Roger was gazing at Mr. Chadburn with a combination of disillusionment and grudging admiration. A lesser man would have tried intimidation or bribery, and put Roger's back up. A lesser man would have made crude threats about taking Roger's profitable egg route away from him. But Mr. Chadburn was too shrewd for that. Instead he appealed to Roger's friendship (after all, Roger did like Mr. Chadburn, and Mrs. Chadburn, and Kiddo Nockamura, too) and his sense of fair play (were they going to let a man like Gilhuly get away with — with a dirty trick?) and his sense of pathos (Mr. Chadburn disgraced, Mrs. Chadburn off to Reno to get a divorce, Kiddo Nockamura sadly returning home to commit *hara-kiri* in his native Japanese village) . . . No wonder Mr. Chadburn was a millionaire financier who made another million dollars every time he went to the city.

With infinite and poignant regret Roger realized what this meant. This meant that no one could ever know he had solved his greatest case. He would have to let the entire village of East Widmarsh go through the rest of its days believing that Inspector Tearle had been unable to discover who had slaughtered Tom, Dick, and Harry. The case would have to go into the files as unsolved.

For one long black moment the situation seemed unbearable. It seemed as dismal as it could possibly have been.

But then a ray of light penetrated.

A thought entered the busy mind of Inspector Tearle, a thought which brought at least partial balm to his suffering.

It also tickled his sense of humor, which was beginning to revive.

He glanced at the master criminal with a new light in his eyes.

"All right, Mr. Chadburn," he said. "I guess our lips are sealed."

A smile burst forth on the miscreant's round face like sunshine on a lagoon.

"Roger, my boy! Now you're talking!"

Kiddo Nockamura darted forward.

"Have more cake! More mirk!"

"It wouldn't be right to ruin everything, when Mr. Gilhuly has been worse than you have," continued Roger, graciously accepting more cake, even though he hadn't finished his first piece.

"That's right, my boy! We can't let Gilhuly get away with it, and I'm glad you can see that."

"*However* . . ." said Roger, toying with his glass of milk. He held it up to the light, observing its rich ivory color. Mr. Chadburn caught his breath. He stared at Roger warily.

"However?" he inquired.

"However," Roger repeated firmly, "I don't think it would be right for Kiddo to get off absolutely scot-free. After all, he *did* kill three geese."

Mr. Chadburn glanced sideways at the impassive face of his cook, and coughed.

"Well . . ."

"And," Roger continued, sipping his milk suavely, "I don't think *you* should get away with it either, Mr. Chadburn. *However* . . ."

"Yes?"

"However, I think we can come to terms . . ."

137

This time Mr. Chadburn gulped. Millionaire financier and chicken-fancier or no millionaire financier and chicken-fancier, he just plain gulped.

"T-terms?" he stammered.

Inspector Tearle nodded.

"Terms!"

The murders had finally been reported to the police, just to get them on the record, and Constable Stubbert was busy trampling the flowers in a fruitless quest for clues.

As for Inspector Tearle, he had other fish to fry. Holding the reins in a masterful way that would have done credit to Old Sarge in his prime, he leaned forward to pat

Thunderbolt's proudly arched neck. Around Roger's waist were Thumbs Thorndyke's arms, and around Thumbs's waist were Shirley's.

"Okay, I guess we've got time for one more ride around the paddock before our cake is ready to come out of the oven. Then we'll take a break while you put on the chocolate frosting and the slivered almonds," he said to Kiddo Nockamura, who was holding Thunderbolt's head by the curb strap of his bridle. "Don't worry, Kiddo. A few more days, and I'll be able to handle Thunderbolt myself, without your having to lead him for us."

"*Shimatta!*" groaned Kiddo Nockamura.

"Giddap!" cried Inspector Tearle.